I0788549

THE IMMORTAL DESCENDANTS ~ BOOK SIX

OUT OF TIME

APRIL WHITE

CORAZON
ENTERTAINMENT

The Immortal Descendants Series
Marking Time
Tempting Fate
Changing Nature
Waging War
Cheating Death
Out of Time

The Immortal Descendants: Baltimore Mysteries
Death's Door

The Baker Street Series
An Urchin of Means

The Cipher Security Series
Code of Conduct
Code of Honor
Code of Matrimony
Code of Ethics

Published by Corazon Entertainment
Palos Verdes Peninsula, CA

Edited by Angela Houle – ahoulebookdoc@gmail.com
© Cover design: FranziskaStern – www.coverdungeon.com –
Instagram: @coverdungeonrabbit

ISBN 978-1-946161-08-6
First American edition, November 2022

"You are the only person who can ever truly determine your worth. No one else has that power unless you give it to them."

~ April White, *An Urchin of Means*

Table of Contents

A Letter to Readers

From April White

When I first met Ringo he was a grubby-capped street urchin whose sole purpose was to be even more street-smart than Saira in a place and time about which she didn't know the rules. The story I'd imagined placed Saira and Archer front and center as the unquestioned heart of everything, but when Ringo told Saira he'd marry her if Archer didn't, my heart slipped right out of my chest and into his hands. However, Ringo had no Immortal Descendant skills and thus, to my mind, no way out of book one. But I didn't count on readers. By the time this book had one hundred reviews, I'd heard from enough people who loved him to realize that I needed to figure out a way to continue Ringo's story.

When I was in college, I was privileged to see the Renaissance Theater Company's production of *King Lear* with Emma Thompson and Kenneth Branagh. Emma Thompson played The Fool — a character whose importance to the story was so much greater than his actual stage time that one forgets exactly how few lines The Fool actually has. She played him as Shakespeare wrote him, wise and witty, playful and yet dead-serious when it mattered. As Ringo took shape in *Marking Time*, he began to echo Emma Thompson's portrayal and became the wisest, most pragmatic character on the page. I'm not spoiling anything when I tell you that his character continues to grow throughout the series (as I hope we all do throughout our lives), because one look at the back-cover copy of the Baker Street Mysteries series should tell you how much Ringo means to me. But because I wrote the Immortal Descendants books (mostly) in Saira's first-person voice, there was never an opportunity to show Ringo's side of things when she wasn't around.

Until now.

The 10th Anniversary editions of the Immortal Descendants series gave me the perfect excuse to make a couple of changes. As you can see, I redesigned the look of the books with these gorgeous covers that perfectly symbolize a family tree, which is at the heart of the Immortal Descendants series. I also did a polish to the manuscript, editing those little things I didn't know I didn't know when I first wrote these books. But perhaps the most value-added change I made is to include a special 10th Anniversary Edition Epilogue from Ringo's point of view at the end of each book. It's the only time in the series that you'll read his thoughts and experience the things that happen to him from his perspective.

It was interesting and challenging to craft these epilogues so long after writing the books, and I made an editorial choice to let go of

Ringo's distinctive accent when he narrates his thoughts and actions for two reasons; first, I don't think in a California accent, so I'm going to hypothesize that Ringo wouldn't think in his accent either, and second, it's frankly too jarring to wade through all the dropped 'h' and 'g' words in his narrative.

This book – *Out of Time* – is where you'll find all those epilogues in one place, along with a bit of a (non-spoiler-ish) summary of where we'd left off with Ringo and/or Charlie in that book. But *Out of Time* has something the Immortal Descendants books don't have – a story about what happened between *Cheating Death* and *An Urchin of Means*. If the epilogues tell of the evolution of Ringo's and Charlie's relationship, *A House Called Home* is the story that bridges the gap between who they were in Victorian London, to who they will become.

I hope you enjoy the extra time spent with Ringo – I do, and I can honestly say, he enjoys hanging out on the page with us too.

Marking Time – A Summary
The Last Time We Saw Ringo

Ringo, Saira, and Archer survived the battle under Bedlam against Bishop Wilder and Jack the Ripper – but not unscathed. They were able to rescue Saira's mother, who had been drained of blood almost to the point of death, but Ringo was forced to kill the Ripper, and Archer was grievously wounded by a Vampire. Saira Clocked them all to safety at the Missus' cottage in Epping Forest, but then had to immediately Clock forward with her mother to get modern medical help, leaving Ringo behind to care for Archer, who was suffering intensely from the effects of his wounds.

Now, several weeks after the porphyria-like infection *turned* Archer, Ringo has been called before the Missus …

Marking Time Epilogue

Choosing Family

"It's time for ye to go home, young Ringo."

"No." I glared at the old woman who meant to send me away from the care and feeding of his Lordship. She saw right through my defiance to the fear underneath, and with her years of being a ma and a grandma, she knocked the defiance right out of me.

"Ye've already done too much." Her tone softened, and my resistance with it. "He's like a child testing his limits right now, and if ye've a mind to be a friend to him, ye can't be the one who sets the limits. It's best ye let him find his way alone for a bit, and when he's chosen his path and set upon it, ye can sidle up and walk beside him as the friend ye are."

"Saira 'ad to leave to save 'er ma, or she'd 'ave been the one to keep 'is Lordship alive. When she left, I promised 'er—" I began, but she cut me off sharply.

"I've seen ye feed him. If ye continue, yer bond with him will be stronger than hers could ever be."

She'd seen me? What else was I supposed to do when his Lordship refused to eat. But what was this about a blood bond?

The Missus continued more gently. "Ye saw how Saira looked at him. Is yer promise worth the risk – to yerself, or to her?"

"Saira's not comin' back," I snapped. I'd always thought that guilt was self-indulgent remorse for bad choices, so it made me testy when it crept up on me.

The Missus scoffed. "This is her mother's time. She has ties here now, and she'll be coming back whether she means to or not."

I refused to let her words lighten the hurt that had wound its way 'round my chest when Saira left. I had no claim on her – not kin, not love – nothing more than friends, but her going left a mark. And I owed something to my friend who was still here.

"'Is Lordship needs—"

"—To heal," the old woman said gently, "and so do ye. Caretaking is just a bandage on loneliness, because when they're done needing ye, the hole they leave behind is sometimes bigger than what ye had to begin with."

"Who says I'm lonely?" My tone held a challenge, but the Missus didn't bite back. She smiled.

"We're all a bit lonely, Ringo, especially the more self-sufficient ones among us. Ye've done well for yerself. Ye've survived, ye've had an adventure, and ye've found people to care about. What ye haven't done yet is let yerself need someone who truly needs ye back."

She handed me a small packet of sandwiches, and I panicked. It was too soon, I wasn't ready to leave this place that felt not quite real, where taking care of his Lordship left no time for thoughts of London and what had happened there. But the Missus patted my hand, and her words were in the quiet tone ye'd use with a skittish beast. I knew I was the beast. "It's time to go home, to a place where ye can sit with the things ye've seen and done. Archer will know where to find ye when he's ready, and so will Saira."

I was being dismissed. She was doing it gently, but she wasn't asking.

I stood reluctantly, already feeling the door close on this place. "I 'ave to say goodbye to 'is Lordship."

She held my arm gently. "He's gone to hunt, and he'll not want ye to see him feed. I'll tell him I sent ye away, and he'll be grateful that ye don't see the shame 'e feels."

"It's not 'is fault," I grumbled, but I knew she was right about his shame. Archer hadn't met my eyes since I'd told him Saira was gone, and it killed a bit more of my spirit each time he looked away.

The Missus pulled me in for a rough hug. "Ye're an intriguing boy, Ringo. I look forward to the interesting man ye'll become."

I caught a ride with a carter to the train station at Chingford, then spent one of the coins Saira had left me for the ticket to London Liverpool Station. I'd never ridden a train as a paying passenger, and the view outside the window gave me something different to focus on – different than the memories that had been stalking most of my waking thoughts and all of my sleeping ones.

I'd killed a man. To be sure, the man himself was a killer, but when I'd taken his life, I became one too. I knew that if the case had gone up before a magistrate, he would've had a time deciding to send me to gaol for stopping the Ripper, But the basic fact was that I'd crossed a line I couldn't step back from. From now to the end of days, my soul would carry a different mark than my early life on the street had left – a mark that wouldn't wash off no matter how hard I scrubbed.

The walk from London Liverpool Station to my hidden flat near the London Bridge was a strange one. I couldn't take the noise of the city after my time in Epping Forest, and the weeks I'd spent tending to Archer had given me a different view on my time as a thief.

I'd been a taker, thinking that the bustle and noise of the city would cover the taking. But in the quiet of the woods, with aught to do but give, I found that the taking didn't fit with the man I wanted to be. I'd seen the sacrifices Saira's da had made for her, and the ones Archer still made. It seemed that love might be the key to becoming a giver. I didn't know if love was in the cards for me, but life as a taker didn't put me any closer to it, so I was done with being a thief. I just hoped I could talk Gosford around to giving me back the job I'd left behind all those weeks ago.

I turned into the alley outside my flat, and another wave of guilt hit me right in the gut. For an ex-thief with no use for guilt, it was becoming entirely too familiar. I'd done a fair job of ignoring the fact that I'd let Charlie, the sister of Mary Kelly, the Ripper's last victim, into my home with a promise of help, and then I'd vanished from London with Saira and Archer, no help at all to someone with nowhere else to turn. But in that alley, where I'd seen Charlie huddled against cold and fear after her sister was murdered, I couldn't ignore my broken promise any longer.

I climbed the ladder to my hidden flat with the dread of wondering – not sure if it was worry that Charlie'd be there or that she wouldn't that made my boots so heavy.

The dread left in a swoop of relief when I saw the slight figure sitting at my table, working by the light of a single candle. She was a bare slip of a thing, pale and skinny, with light eyes and fair hair, but there was something a bit more substantial to Charlie now. Maybe it was less fear, or more security, or maybe those things were in me and I saw her through different eyes. She looked up in surprise at my entrance, and then stood so suddenly that she had to grab for her chair before it crashed to the floor. "Ye've come back," she said, nearly breathless, setting the chair to rights.

"I 'ave," I agreed. The edgy, unsettled feeling I'd carried on my walk home didn't come in with me, and my flat was warmer and more inviting than I'd ever known it to be.

"I'll be goin' then," she said, gathering up a pencil and bit of paper from the table.

"Charlie," I said in a voice I hoped was gentle. Her eyes seemed too big for her face, and the quick, bird-like movements stilled while she waited for me to say what I would. I honestly had no idea what I meant to say, and the words that came out startled me as much as her. "You should stay 'ere."

"Why?" she asked. It was a question I didn't rightly know the answer to.

I stepped farther into the room. I could see Charlie's instinct to step back, but she held her ground, impressing me with strength I didn't expect.

"Saira and I said before that we'd be yer family if ye wanted it—"

Charlie's gaze shifted hopefully to the ladder behind me. I understood that look because I'd worn it enough the past few weeks to know the hurt that would come with it.

"She's … gone," I said. The words were surprisingly hard to put voice to, and I cleared my throat to say the rest. "And I'm finding myself short a flatmate."

She studied me in silence and to let her, I turned my eyes to the small changes in the attic room. Drawings of fanciful creatures in a delicate hand were tacked to the wall opposite the bathtub. The creatures came alive on the page and could have been drawings from one of the books Archer had brought in, except I recognized none of them. Pictures had made learning the words easier, and when Archer'd figured out my shortcut, he made sure every book he brought was full of them.

Thoughts of his Lordship ached, so I distracted myself by looking for other changes. There was a slightly tattered hooked rug that covered the floor near the big armchair where Charlie must have been sleeping. She was small enough that it likely wasn't a hardship, where I'd been cramped and uncomfortable when Saira had used the bed. It seemed that Saira and Archer still laid claim to my memories of home, and I'd do well to smile through them instead of wincing.

A bit of rosemary was potted by the window, and a chipped tea mug held strands of ivy. There were two pegs on a post near the ladder where a coat Archer had left behind hung next to a much smaller jumper, likely the only warm thing Charlie had to wear.

When she finally spoke again, the words were quiet. "There's a bit of fish pie left over if ye're 'ungry."

I nodded, relieved to have something simple to turn my attention to. "I'll never say no to a bite to eat."

She motioned for me to sit, then put a plate down in front of me. The crust had gone cold, but the fish and onions in rich gravy were still warm and tasted better than anything in the shops. "Ye didn't steal this?" I asked, suddenly suspicious of her survival skills.

"I made it," she said with a scowl, "and ye can give it right back if ye're goin' to call me a thief." The tart tone was much better than the whispered one, and I was oddly glad I could get a rise out of her. She reached for the bowl, but I wrapped my arm around it protectively.

"I didn't know ye could cook," I said, taking another bite with no kind of apology.

"There's a lot ye don't know about me." She glared at me, and the fierceness looked interesting on her.

"So sit down and tell me somethin' then," I scowled right back. "For example, 'ow 'ave ye been keepin' yerself fed?"

She eyed me warily, and then finally sat across the small table while I scraped the bottom of my bowl clean.

"Work, same as always. I was apprentice to a seamstress before Mary …" her voice trailed off. "Yer man Gosford let me work yer job 'till ye came back," Charlie finally said, "and 'e gives me a fish every other day. 'E also buys the odd sketch from me for 'is baby granddaughter."

I looked at her in surprise. "The sketches are yours then?"

She gave a quick nod and then waved my question away like it wasn't the point. 'E came lookin' for ye when ye'd been missin' for a few days, so 'e'll be glad yer 'ome safe." Charlie peered at me with a frown. "Ye are safe, aren't ye?"

I nodded, avoiding her eyes and the question. Sure, I was safe – safely home eating fish pie while one friend battled himself, and another fought to save her mother's life. I'd also killed a man, and it was that thought that finally made me meet her gaze. "The Ripper's dead."

Whatever she'd thought I was about to say, it wasn't that.

"I killed him," I said, needing to lay the words out for her to judge.

She held my eyes before she finally nodded again. "Thank ye." The sharpness had gone from her tone, and what was left sounded fragile. "I might finally be able to sleep now."

"Ye 'ad nightmares?" I asked.

She exhaled, and her eyes darted toward the bed. "Every night."

I'd seen the room she'd shared with her sister. Charlie had been there the night the Ripper came calling, with no place to hide except under the bed where Mary plied her trade, and where she died. The horrors in my own memory were bad enough, I couldn't imagine what Charlie saw when she closed her eyes against the dark.

I wiped my mouth and stood to clean my plate. "It's another reason for ye to stay. There's safety in numbers, even from dreams."

"I'd like to feel safe," she said quietly, trying the words as if they were a new language.

I had only understood safety a couple of years before, when I'd found my home in the hidden attic above an accountancy office, and it was something I'd learned how to share since Saira and Archer had stumbled into my life. There was safety in numbers, but more than that, there was comfort in sharing experiences. Things seemed less dire when someone else knew what you'd been through.

I nodded, as though that was settled. "Ye're a good cook. I'll trade ye readin' lessons for cookin' ones."

Her eyes widened in surprise, like she hadn't considered that she brought anything of value into our living arrangement. And then she smiled, and it was like watching the first, wobbly flight of a baby bird — fear turning to confidence, 'till her face was full of joy.

"Ye 'ave yerself a deal," she said in a tone that sounded stronger and more sure. "I've been lookin' at yer books, and I want to start with this one." She handed me an illustrated copy of *Alice's Adventures in Wonderland.*

We'd been out walking one evening, Saira, Archer, and me, and we'd passed a bookseller in Marylebone with children's stories in the window. Saira'd called the books "old," and she couldn't take her eyes off them. When she'd admitted she'd never actually read that one, Archer'd bought it for her as a present.

We read it together, the three of us, taking it in turns. Sometimes, after Archer read his chapter, Saira would talk about her mum, about how Alice's fall down the rabbit hole must've been what her mum felt going forward in time, where everything was strange and she was all alone.

And then she'd reach for Archer's hand, and she'd nudge me with a foot, and she'd tell us that no matter how strange this time was, she'd never felt alone. "And now you're stuck with me," she'd said, and I wished for that more than I knew how to say.

But I wasn't alone either. A fierce, frightened orphan girl sat across my table, waiting for me to keep my end of a bargain I'd made with no notion as to why I'd made it. Maybe it was because I'd been alone for so long, and then I wasn't anymore. I knew what alone felt like, and I didn't want to go back.

I opened the book, and inside the cover was an inscription I'd never seen before. It was in Saira's hand.

Ringo,

There's family you're born to, and family you choose.

Thank you for being my family.

Love, Saira

"Ye alright?" Charlie asked in her small voice. The smile had gone from her face, and suddenly I wanted to put it back.

I cleared my throat and took a shaky breath. "Yeah. I will be."

Then I wiped the shine from my eye and began to read.

Tempting Fate – A Summary
The Last Time We Saw Ringo

During their adventures in Tudor times, Ringo became closer to Saira and Archer than ever, and reuniting with them as they prevented a split in the time stream was like rejoining the family he never knew he needed. But when he followed Saira to the future and the past, he left behind Charlie, the part-Clocker sister of the Ripper's last victim who had become his flatmate and friend. With Saira, he saw horrors, fought demons, and experienced wonders he never could have imagined possible, and in the process, he grew up more in the month he was gone than in his entire life before that point. Everything changed.

And now it is time to go home.

TEMPTING FATE EPILOGUE
GOING HOME

"Ye're back," Charlie whispered, as if she couldn't quite believe I'd just walked into my flat.

I had swiped my tears away before I'd started up the ladder, determined to leave the past behind and step back into my life, but my voice broke when I said, "Ye're surprised?"

Walking away from Saira on the street hadn't been easy, but I'd done it without looking back, so something about Charlie's disbelief rankled, especially as it was so good to see her. She wore the simple skirt and blouse combination she favored at home, and her fair hair was pulled to one side in a casual braid, like always. Her skin had a bit of pink in it from time spent in the sun, and her waif-like figure might have grown a bit taller, but otherwise she looked familiar and comfortable. She looked like home.

With everything I'd experienced in both the future and the past, familiar and comfortable were worth a fair bit, and I couldn't put a price to being home.

But then Charlie shrugged like it didn't matter, and some of my relief at finding her there dimmed. "Ye went to the future," she said. "I thought for sure ye'd find more things to interest ye there than are 'ere."

I frowned. "It doesn't work like that. I can't just stay in a time that isn't my own. There are rules, and breakin' them can 'ave bigger consequences than just bein' out of place."

I was so tired. Even the short rest I'd taken in Saira's tower room at St. Brigid's hadn't restored me to myself. I'd had so few hours of sleep my body didn't even shut down properly anymore – it just … stopped. I was afraid to sit on the bed to kick off my boots because I wouldn't even get the laces untied before I dropped. I must've swayed, because Charlie was across the room, with her shoulder under my arm before I could even think to support myself.

"Come," she said. Her voice had softened, and she led me to my bed. I swayed again, and she put a small hand on my chest and pushed. "Lie down. Ye look ready to fall asleep on yer feet. I'll 'elp ye get yer boots off …" Her voice trailed off as she studied my feet.

"They're Saira's," I mumbled as my eyes closed.

"Of course they are," Charlie murmured.

I might have questioned her tone if I'd stayed awake long enough to form the words.

I slept through to the next morning, while Charlie went to the docks and was home before I knew she'd been gone. Gosford told her to let me sleep, but he'd be expecting me at dawn the next day. Charlie gave me the message, then said nothing else while she fried a fish in butter with some of the sage she had growing in a pot on the window ledge. She put two plates of fish on the table, and it smelled better than anything I'd eaten in weeks.

We ate in a silence that became loud the longer it went on. Finally, I put my fork down and looked at her. "Don't ye want to know what 'appened?"

She avoided my eyes and said, "If ye want to tell me," then stood up to clear our plates.

I wanted to tell her everything. I wanted to share every sight, every sound and smell and taste from Saira's time, and also Milady's time. I wanted to marvel over the machines that made pictures move and talk, and I wanted to hear her gasps of shock and horror and delight at my tales of swordfights and deadly plots.

But Charlie was intent on holding herself apart from me, and I might as well tell my tales to the walls. I sighed and reached for the dishes. "Ye cooked, I'll clean," I said, not letting go of the plates when she'd have taken them from me.

She filled the basin while I scrubbed the cast iron pan with rock salt, then I carried everything up to the roof to wash. I didn't understand her silence, but it felt thick and heavy, and when the dishes were put away I put the kettle on. She'd retreated to the chair she slept in, so I wandered the loft while I waited for the water to boil.

There were new drawings pinned to the walls, and I admired the charcoal shading Charlie had started using to highlight the little magical creatures that hid throughout her street scenes. One of the new pieces, a scene of a gang of thugs breaking into a print shop, stopped me in my tracks. I knew those lads. It was Lizzer's gang, but … not. Some of them were just as I'd last seen them, of course. The same dirty clothes and worn shoes, with sneers on gaunt faces and ropes holding torn trousers up on bony hips. But two of them looked nothing like the boys I knew from my old gang. Spins had pointy ears, fingers as long as his forearms, and teeth filed to sharp tips, and Lizzer … Lizzer looked like a walking dead man, pale and nearly skeletal under his trademark bowler hat.

"What is this?" I asked Charlie, pointing at the new drawing. "It wasn't 'ere before."

"Just somethin' I drew," she said, lookin' away from me.

"This isn't like the others." Uncertainty made me testy, and my tone was sharper than I liked. "The creatures aren't cute brownies and sprites and whatnot like ye usually draw."

She shrugged and wouldn't meet my eyes.

"Do ye know them?" I asked.

She must've heard the edge in my voice because she looked up sharply. "No."

"Charlie," My voice was deadly calm, "I know those lads, and I need to know where ye saw them and what," I inhaled, "they are."

She stared at me, 'er eyes fixed on mine like a mouse hypnotized by a snake. I waited for her to say something, anything that made sense, but no words came out, just the sound of quick breaths, and the pulse racing in her throat.

Charlie was terrified, and the idea that it was me she was afraid of was what finally knocked the temper off me. I exhaled, broke eye contact, and pointed to Lizzer. "If ye didn't already know, that's Lizzer. Ye knew I was dodgin' 'im when I left London, I just didn't realize ye … actually knew 'im."

She finally spoke, and I breathed easier for the sound of her voice, even if the words made me want to spit nails. "I don't know 'im, I swear. They followed me 'ome one day. They were roughin' each other 'round, like they were playin', but each time one of 'em made a grab for another, they got closer and closer to me."

I looked steadily at her, more afraid of the answer than I had words for. "And did they catch ye?"

She gave a quick shake of her head. "I was comin' 'ome from Gosford's boat, dressed in some of yer old clothes. When I knew they were after me, I walked straight up to a carter, climbed into the seat next to 'im, and 'anded 'im the fish I was carryin'. The man was so surprised 'e just took the fish with a nod, and next thing 'e knew, I'd jumped down and run away past 'is cart. That lot," she said, nodding toward the drawing of Lizzer's gang, "was lookin' for an easy target, and I made things complicated with the carter."

"Ye did right," I exhaled, "especially if they didn't see where ye went."

"They didn't," she said quietly.

The edge of sharp anger still churned in my belly, and I worked to keep it from my tone. "'E thinks family and loved ones are fair game, and if 'e knows 'e can 'urt me by goin' after ye, 'e won't stop."

She stared at me, clearly surprised by something I'd said, but since she stayed silent, I studied the drawing again. "Why'd ye draw 'im like somethin' that crawled out of the ground? I'm not sayin' ye're wrong—"

"'E's a wight," she said fast, like she was ripping off a bandage stuck to a wound.

"A what?" I asked. Her tone had almost been frantic, like saying the word was as frightening as whatever it meant.

"A wight. It's one of the *other* … kind, not exactly among the livin', but not … not truly alive either."

Things that didn't make sense were starting to become my stock in trade, so her answer didn't surprise me. But knowing a thing was different than understanding it. "So, yer sayin' a wight is a real thing, Lizzer is one, and ye can see it on 'im like ye can see the brownies and pixies and whatnot?"

She nodded, eyes wide again like she was back to being afraid. Or maybe it was all just degrees of fear with her if she could see things like wights. I pointed to the drawing again. "What's Spins then?"

"Fae," she whispered.

Huh.

"I've seen yer drawin's of fae before, and they're like the fairies that dance around on mushroom caps in the forest. Spins isn't that."

She shook her head. "Those are brownies pretendin' to be fae. 'E's one of the Unseelie."

Charlie said the word as if saying it would conjure something she'd rather not, so I took it to mean Spins was something deeply unpleasant. This wasn't news to me – he was a ratty bit of guttersnipe when he wasn't pure nastiness, torturing the young ones.

I scowled, then realized Charlie still wasn't meeting my eyes. "Ye've told me about the 'armless things, but ye left out the nasties. I want to 'ear about *all* the things ye can see, and then I want to tell ye the things I've seen in the future *and* the past."

She finally looked up and met my eyes, her expression hopeful and wary at the same time. "You're not angry?"

That genuinely startled me. "Angry about what? I'm plenty angry that Lizzer and 'is gang o' creatures followed ye, but that's not what ye mean, is it?"

"My mother taught me never to talk about what I could see," Charlie said softly. "I might've been testin' ye with the 'armless ones," she held my gaze for a bit before looking away, "but the others … Ma said people turn mean when they're scared. I'd be called a liar, or worse."

"Well, only a fool wouldn't believe ye, and I've never 'ad the luxury of bein' foolish," I held her gaze. "But ye were talkin' about fear, and maybe even wonderin' what it looks like on me." She hesitated, then nodded, so I continued. "To my way of thinkin', bein' scared maybe adds a bit more speed when I'm runnin', or a bit of quick thinkin' when I 'ave a choice to make. My 'eart pounds a little, and maybe I sweat, but fear can be fun too." A half-smile quirked up my lip. "Sometimes it's just a body's way of sayin' *well, this is new, 'ow are ye goin' to deal with it?*"

"That happened to me with the wight's gang and the carter. Everythin' just got really clear, and it was only afterwards that the shakin' started." She frowned in thought. "But men are different. Annie always said fear makes 'em angry."

I shrugged casually instead of wrapping her up in protective wool like I suddenly had a mind to. "That's probably more true than not, but I can only speak for myself. I'm not scared of bein' afraid. It doesn't feel so very different than bein' excited, and it's definitely not somethin' to get angry about."

She still hesitated, so I held out my hand to her. "Come, we're goin' to share yer chair, because the rest of this conversation's goin' to take a while and it's the most comfortable seat in the place." I took one side of the big armchair and patted the seat next to me. "Sometimes it's easier to talk side-by-side instead of lookin' at each other."

She smiled reluctantly and crawled into the chair. I put my arm around her slender shoulders, and was happy she didn't stiffen and pull away. We were friends and flatmates, but we'd been careful to give each other space to call our own. I was crowding her space by sitting in the chair with her, and I hoped that maybe she didn't mind.

"Put yer 'ead on my chest then," I said, trying to sound like I was being practical. "Listen to my 'eart while ye tell yer story. It gets faster when I'm runnin', or when I want to run, so ye'll know what scares me."

She looked up at me, maybe to see if I was serious, and then slowly, carefully, she laid her head on my chest. I huffed a laugh at myself.

"'Course, my 'eart could speed up for other reasons too, I guess." Even as I said the words, I felt the pounding of my heart like it was a drum. I could smell the soap she made with rosemary and a bit of lemon peel, and my fingers found their way to the silky braid she wore over her shoulder. The plaited hair slipped through my fingers as I played with the pattern, and the longer she didn't pull away, the harder my heart beat, until I felt it in my blood.

"I thought yer 'eart belonged to Saira," Charlie finally said. "Ye're wearin' 'er boots."

Was that it? The reason she'd been distant? Could she be … jealous?

The sound I made was between a scoff and a laugh. "I'm currently sittin' in yer bed with ye, but the circumstances don't mean anythin' without intent." I took a breath, because I was suddenly very aware that we were, in fact, side by side on Charlie's bed. I let go of her braid and tried to focus. "Saira and Archer, they're family – the kind ye love no matter 'ow ye feel about them that day or the next." She allowed the weight of her head to rest back on my chest, and a deep sense of contentment stole over me. "They're in my 'eart, but they don't 'ave it." My words were murmured against Charlie's hair. I wanted to pull her even closer, curl her into my lap and anchor myself with her.

"So, yer 'eart, it might be up for grabs then?" she asked, and I wondered if there was a tiny smile in the sound of her voice.

"Depends who's doin' the grabbin'," I said, hearing my own smile.

This time I felt her grin against my shirt, and my heart thumped even louder. I laughed at myself, tugged her closer to me, and rested my chin on the top of her head. "Now, tell me about all the nasty creatures ye can see, and 'ow ye know what they're called, and don't leave anythin' out. And after ye've properly scared me with all the bogeymen in the world, I'll tell ye a story about a princess in a tower, and an evil bishop who wanted 'er blood."

Charlie wrapped her arm around my waist and snuggled in with a sigh. "Bogeymen will only come after ye if ye've done somethin' evil right in front of them. It's a barghest ye must watch for. They're the quiet ones who do their 'untin' in dark alleys."

I shivered and gave in to the temptation to pull Charlie's legs across my lap so I could hold her in both arms. I'd never considered being so bold before, but torture and near-death in my recent experiences had managed to take the edge off my sense of propriety. And then I realized how right she felt in my arms.

"I'm clearly not meant to be walkin' out without ye to spot the nasties and warn me." I was trying to sound as light and unconcerned as usual, but the only thing I could think about was the softness of her skin, and the way her hair smelled of herbs and summer and home.

She nestled into my arms, and my heart calmed so much I wondered if something was wrong. But I felt the opposite of wrong, and I surrendered to the peace she brought me.

"I don't know about what's meant or not," she said quietly. "I'm not sure I believe there's a reason for things bein' the way they are, or things like murdered sisters and evil bishops and princesses in towers."

"What *are* ye sure of?" I asked, suddenly wanting to know the answer more than anything.

She hesitated, and I didn't want her to be uncertain. I opened my mouth to go first – to maybe make it safe for her to share something of herself – but she beat me to the words.

"I'm sure," she breathed, her voice getting bolder, "that believin' a thing is *meant to be* takes away some of the magic of it. Me walkin' beside ye any time, whether I'm warnin' ye of creatures or not, is … magical. It's ye choosin' me, and me choosing ye, even for that moment, and there's so much magic in that I almost burst with the feelin' of it."

She'd spoken to my chest, her eyes never meeting mine, and it was like she whispered a secret to my heart. Then she pulled back to look at me.

"Yer 'eart is beating so fast. Did I scare ye?"

How had I never noticed how bright her eyes were? How curious and cautious they were, and how carefully she searched my face. I could read whole sentences in her eyes, whole novels full of hope and pain, fear and trust, laughter and love.

"My 'eart's answerin' ye the only way it knows 'ow, so I'll try to translate the feelin' into words," I finally said. "I do feel scared, yeah? Scared of the tiny, precious bundle of carin' I'm holdin' like it's a newborn babe, all messy and unformed and just as likely to scream and cry as to nestle in for warmth and comfort." Her small giggle escaped with just enough volume for me to hear, and I had to resist trying to make her laugh. I loved her laugh, but I needed her to believe me. "I've 'ad friends, sure. Good friends I'd just as soon die for as see 'urt. But I've never known someone to care about as my own. I'm scared

I'll mess up, do or say somethin' wrong, not be strong enough or worthy. So yeah, I'm scared."

Her eyes flicked back and forth on mine, like she was weighing my words. I trapped her gaze with my own and held it so she could see that I meant what I said. "But I'm not gearin' up to run. It's like ye said, what I'm lookin' at just seems really clear. And this—" I gestured between us, "what we could 'ave between us – it's big and important and it's so full of everythin' possible *I* almost burst with the feelin' of it. I've never felt that before – for anyone – but I'm not scared of it if ye're by my side."

Carefully, almost like she was finding the courage, she lifted her hand and touched my face. Her fingertips barely grazed my cheek, but I felt the contact like it was fire dancing across my skin. Then, so slowly I nearly died anticipating it, her hand reached around to the back of my neck. With the tiniest pressure she pulled me toward her, her eyes on mine first, then slipping down to my mouth.

I was nearly afraid to breathe – not wanting to do anything to break her concentration as she gently pulled herself up to meet my lips with hers. Her breath whispered against mine until, with the most tentative touch, she kissed me. My fingers twitched convulsively, wanting to draw her tightly to me, but I needed her to lead this.

Her touch grew confident, and she pressed herself into me until her fingers were threaded through my hair, and what had been a soft exploration became insistent and bold.

Ten minutes or seconds or years later, she pulled back just far enough that I had to force my eyes up from her lips. They were shiny with tears, and my arms clenched around her reflexively.

"Tell me," I said, my heartbeat suddenly anxious.

"I've always known there was magic out in the world," she said, smiling as I wiped a tear from her cheek. "Ye make me feel it inside myself."

And then my heart did burst into a thousand bits, and she gathered them all up and held them in her hands.

Changing Nature – A Summary
The Last Time We Saw Ringo and Charlie

After the time stream was repaired, Saira, with the help of Charlie and Lady Valerie, transported Archer, Ringo, and Connor back to the island in the middle of the Seine in Paris in 1429. There was unfinished business with Wilder to take care of, though, and Ringo would not leave Saira and Archer to do it alone.

Lady Valerie asked Charlie to come home to 1554 with her. She would take her to court and teach her to be a lady, and Charlie's presence would help distract Lady Valerie from the pain of losing her only son. Ringo had a heartfelt conversation with Charlie before he left the island with Saira and Archer, and he wouldn't discuss what had been said with either of them. Connor, emotionally and physically exhausted after battling Joan of Arc, stayed on the island with Lady Valerie and Charlie, but when Saira, Archer, and Ringo finally returned with Tom, battered and nearly broken, Connor was there alone. Charlie and Lady Valerie had gone.

Though Ringo was unhappy about Charlie's absence, he refused Saira's offer to bring Charlie back from 1554, saying that she'd chosen her life, and so had he – and until the mixed-bloods were found and the Monger ring destroyed, his place was next to Saira and Archer.

When they returned to the present, they found tensions at St. Brigid's high, and the missing mixed-bloods had yet to be found. Ringo remained at Elian Manor with Saira, Archer, and Connor's family – protected from the Mongers, and waiting for their next move.

Changing Nature Epilogue
Courage

"She said you told her to leave." Connor's voice was carefully neutral as I sat next to him on the stone wall that separated an old apple orchard from the woods at the end of Elian Manor's land. He didn't look at me, and I wondered if maybe his Wolf didn't want the words to be a challenge. Come to think of it, he hadn't been meeting my eyes much in the days since we'd come back from France.

"Ye'll need to be more specific," I said with more edge than I meant to.

"You send a lot of girls away, do you?" He scoffed, and turned to face me. There was just enough yellow in his eyes that I looked away. My instinct to stay alive hadn't taken damage in the hunt for Wilder, even if nothing else felt quite whole.

"She wanted to go. I just made it easier for 'er to leave," I said with a shrug that could have meant anything. Connor's eyes narrowed at me.

Just beyond the wall, where the field ended in a small wood, the late afternoon sun patterned the ground with shadows and light. I hopped down off the stones and walked into the dappled shade where a small patch of wildflowers grew. They were blue cornflowers, and they called to mind the color of Charlie's eyes, so I sat with my back against a tree and watched them dance with the shifting light. I needed the distance from Connor's glare as much as I wanted the connection with something that reminded me of her.

Apparently the distance was enough, because when my young friend joined me on the grass, his eyes were back to normal, whatever that was now.

"She cried when she left with Lady Valerie," he said. "I think maybe she felt like she wasn't … enough for you."

I scowled. "Did she say that?"

He plucked at a blade of grass. "She didn't have to."

"Then 'ow did ye come to be such an expert on Charlie?" I didn't like the sick feeling of regret that had crept in with Connor's words.

He shrugged. "Not Charlie. Not really. I mostly just know what it's like to have big shoes to fill, to wonder if you're up to the task."

I stared at him. "What shoes does Charlie 'ave to fill but 'er own?"

He huffed. "Come on, Ringo. You don't think she wonders if she could ever be interesting or strong enough to be more to you than Saira is?"

"What's Saira got to do with anythin'?"

Connor shrugged. "She's the human equivalent of an alpha wolf, and Charlie thinks she's a submissive, which is why her feelings were hurt that you sent her away."

"Do I 'ave to say it again? I didn't send 'er away," I said through gritted teeth.

"You did," he said. "At least that's how she heard it."

"Why are ye tellin' me this, Connor?" I snapped. "What's done is done, and I can't undo it now." The regret was growing, and I wanted to be done with the conversation.

This time, his eyes held mine without blinking. "Because maybe, if you're lucky, you'll have a chance to do better next time."

He walked away then without looking back, and I didn't follow him, hoping the regret would depart with him.

It didn't.

I tried to hide from my thoughts for a few hours, but they were loud and nagged like a burr in a wool sock. I finally went in search of Connor to at least rid myself of the guilt of having snapped at him.

He wasn't in the makeshift lab, where he'd taken to working with his uncle, and he wasn't in the library, which was my favorite place to hide, so I tried the flat over the garage where he lived with his mum, Liz, and his younger brother and sister.

When little Sophie let me into the flat, Liz popped her head out from the kitchen, waving a wooden spoon in my direction.

"Ringo, the boys are out, and Claire has allergies, so her nose is useless. I need your taste buds. Come and tell me if this stew has enough—" she waved the spoon airily "—of whatever it is lamb stew needs."

I followed her into the kitchen where Saira's mum, Claire, sat at the table, with a box of tissue next to her. I greeted them both and then obligingly took the spoonful of meat and potatoes that Liz held out for me. It was good – rich with a tomato broth – but it lacked the depth of flavor that made Charlie's cooking special.

"There's rosemary, thyme, and some chives outside," I said. "Mind if I add some?"

"Have at it," she said with a wave in the general direction of the pot that bubbled on the stove. "The potatoes and carrots are fresh from the garden, but I'm winging it with the rest."

I gathered herbs I knew from the ones Charlie had kept at our flat, and others I'd seen her buy from a man in the market she said was part Druid, and then set about mincing everything and adding it along with more salt and some of the dried spices Liz had that smelled interesting. The result, according to my taste buds and hers, was exactly right.

"You're a genius, Ringo. Thank you." Liz gave the pot a final stir and set the lid back on for it to stew.

"The credit goes to Charlie. She taught me which plants to add to make things interestin'."

"Saira said she's gone to the Tudor court?" Liz asked. I glanced over at Claire, whose expression was sad as she leaned back in her chair and sipped her tea. She and Charlie had gotten close in the short time they'd known each other, but Charlie's absence wasn't something Claire and I had talked about.

Liz nudged the cookie tin toward me and I helped myself with a "thank you" as I answered her. "Lady Valerie said she'd be at court just long enough to say 'er goodbyes before she leaves for 'er country estate. I imagine Charlie will do things she'd never 'ave dreamt about as a girl on the streets."

"Was that not true for the time she spent here as well?" Claire said softly as she watched me over the rim of her mug. I shrugged.

"For me it is, but apparently not for 'er."

"Did she ask you if she should go, or did she tell you she was leaving?" Liz asked with the kind of precision I'd heard her son wield.

I exhaled. "She asked if she should go with Lady Valerie."

"And?" Liz asked gently.

"I told 'er she should do what she wanted, and not to stay on my account." I sounded defensive, and wondered if I'd sounded the same way when I'd said the words to Charlie.

Claire winced, but Liz smiled and her tone was soft and kind. "At which point she had no choice but to go."

"How do ye figure?" I thought I did a pretty decent job of keeping the scowl out of my tone, but Claire's arched eyebrow told another tale.

"It's human nature, Ringo," Liz said. I realized that both she and Claire had lost husbands, but maybe more important to the conversation, they were both women that Charlie admired. So did I.

"To be strong and confident in our own eyes," Liz continued, "we need to feel that our choices are our own. Her mistake was to ask your advice about whether she should go. If she had just stayed or just gone, you'd never have had a say in the decision, and her appearance of self-confidence could have remained intact."

I wanted to throw my hands up in frustration. "So I shouldn't have answered at all?"

Just then, a Sparrow darted into the kitchen through the open window and settled on the back of a kitchen chair. Liz barely hesitated before she spoke to it. "You can just fly right to your room, young man. We have guests, and they don't need to be treated to your bare backside along with the tea."

The Sparrow chittered at her but flew out of the room.

"Logan?" Claire asked Liz.

She sighed the sound of the long-suffering. "My dramatic child."

Logan charged back into the kitchen wearing a pair of flannel pajama bottoms and nothing else. "Mum!" He was breathless with urgency. "Connor is sulking in the woods and won't come back with me for anything."

"Is he now," Liz said, sliding a cookie over to her youngest son and removing the plate from his grasp. "Dinner's almost ready. He'll come back for that."

"No he won't," Logan wailed. "He said he wasn't even hungry."

Liz met my eyes. "Will you stay to dinner, Ringo?"

"I …sure?" I wasn't at all sure Connor would want me to be there, but I'd come to find him after all.

She nodded and turned briskly to Logan. "Tell him Ringo's here."

Logan looked at me with a scowl. "He's mad at you. He won't come."

"He's not mad, he's hurt," Liz said.

I flinched at the truth of her words, then looked Logan in the eyes. "Would ye tell 'im I came to apologize."

"What'd you do?" he demanded.

"Connor said some things to me that made me feel like a rotten 'uman bein', so I punished him by actin' like one."

"Your brother will come so he and Ringo can talk through whatever they need to," Liz said, "but only if you tell him he's here." She waved her hand at Logan to shoo.

"You guys are weird," Logan declared as he shoved the rest of the cookie into his mouth with one big bite, "talking when you could race or wrestle or run until someone throws up."

Logan rolled his eyes and then exploded into a yellow Parakeet and flew out the window. I watched him go with amused wonder as Liz scooped up the fallen pajama bottoms with a sigh.

"I've tried runnin' until I throw up," I said with a shake of my head. "It never works."

Liz left the room chuckling, and I took the seat next to Claire. "How could I have answered differently when Charlie asked what I thought about 'er goin' back with Lady Valerie?"

"You could have said, 'I support you in whatever choice you make, for whatever reason you make it,' but only if you genuinely did," she said, as Liz re-entered the kitchen, minus the pajamas. "If you wanted her to choose one way or the other, you could have been honest about that as well."

"She'd 'ave stayed if I'd said I wanted 'er to, but that's wrong."

"Wrong because you think she'd be subverting her own desire to yours, or wrong because you'd feel guilty asking her to stay if she wanted to go?"

I scowled. "Makes it sound like I think she's weak. She 'as one of the biggest and strongest 'earts I know."

"Then trust her. Trust that she actually did want to go or she'd have stayed behind," Liz chimed in with a certainty I struggled to feel.

Claire reached out and touched my hand. "I know exactly how hard it is to care for someone whose journey is different than your own."

I frowned. "Yer 'usband was committed to an asylum. That's not so much a journey as a destination, no?"

Her smile deepened the lines just beginning to form around her eyes. "I'm talking about my daughter. About all of you, actually. Your lives are taking you to places and experiences I've never even imagined, and you come back changed by things I can't even fathom. But I don't have to understand *why* you are to love *who* you are."

"I can see that it could be that way for you with Saira," I said. "She's yer daughter. A mother's supposed to love 'er child no matter what."

"Ringo—" Claire met my eyes and held my gaze with her own while she searched for words. "Love is mysterious, but it is also intentional. When we choose to love, we can love through thick and thin, pain and joy, in sickness and in health, and even across time." She smiled softly and added, "which is another thing you and I have in common."

"Did ye ever …" I cleared the gob of feelin' from my throat and tried again. "When ye went back to visit Saira's da, did ye ever feel like too much 'ad changed? Like ye weren't the same person ye were when ye loved 'im? Like maybe 'e wouldn't know ye anymore?"

She touched my cheek gently. "When I say love is intentional, that's exactly what I mean. No matter what had changed or who we'd become in the times between my visits, I looked forward to relearning his laugh, his smile, the way he looked at me, the scent of his skin, and all the things, big and small, that had become part of him. There were times it was uncomfortable, and other times when it felt just like pulling on warm socks over cold feet, but it became as much a part of our routine as morning tea or holding hands had been when we were together every day."

I absorbed Claire's words along with the comforting scents of Liz's stew, the sounds of the tea kettle, the knife on the chopping board, and the feeling of *home* the kitchen and these women inspired. "I've been thinkin' of love like it's a magic spell that might find me and someone else and weave us together, if we're lucky. Like it's some mix of mystery and alchemy sprinkled with pixie dust that left me breathless and tongue-tied and unsure of my own name." I chuckled and shook my head at myself. "It makes no sense, because I've seen Saira and Archer work through all the bits and pieces and pains of lovin' each other, but I 'adn't really considered that I didn't 'ave to leave it to magic and chance. If I wanted it, and she wanted it, we could write our own love story."

Claire Elian smiled at me. "If you want it, and she wants it, you *will* write your own love story."

Waging War – A Summary
The Last Time We Saw Ringo

In 1944, Archer vanished into the rubble of the British Museum Underground Station after the V-1 bomb exploded. Despondent, Saira and Ringo said a heartfelt goodbye to Rachel and left her in Ringo's flat when they Clocked to the present.

But it wasn't the present they expected.

Elian Manor had been abandoned since the 1960s. Millicent had married her pilot, and her grandchildren were Clockers at St. Brigid's School. Friends had become wary, Mongers were toothless, Mr. Shaw was hostile and suspicious, and even Ms. Simpson wanted Saira and Ringo to leave. Everything was wrong because *time had split*.

Archer had never occupied the St. Brigid's cellars on the new timeline, and surprisingly, it was Saira's infuriating "cousin" Doran who offered the first glimmer of hope – Archer didn't exist on the new timeline because he'd died in the explosion in 1944, but there *was* a timeline on which he did exist.

We left Saira and Ringo on the alternate time stream in the Clocker Tower at St. Brigid's just as the fall term was beginning. They knew they needed to find a way to repair the time stream if they were to have any hope of finding the future in which Archer lived.

And though Saira and Ringo have talked about Ringo's feelings for Charlie, we haven't seen Charlie since 1429 when she left Paris with Lady Valerie …

WAGING WAR EPILOGUE
CHARLIE – GRAYSON MANOR, 1554

The sun blazed overhead, and the heavy gown I'd worn over hose and tunic in order to escape the manor house lay abandoned on the grass. Escape was perhaps not the right word, as I hadn't left the property and had no knowledge of whether I even could, given that my ability to go back to my own time was completely out of my hands. I was essentially trapped in the 16th century, though it was a gilded cage of my own choosing, and as such, I took my freedoms where I could. On this warm summer day, freedom from the weight of velvet and brocade was pushing the boundaries of respectability, but until my art teacher arrived, I could stay out of sight of the manor house in the surrounding wood.

I took aim at a bit of red silk tacked to a tree. The arrow nocked in my bow was one of the set my friend, Christian de Cardenas, had made for me.

"Aim slightly high and to the left," Christian said from the shade of a nearby tree. "If you listen carefully, you can hear the rustle of the leaves from the breeze that will spoil a straight shot."

I adjusted my aim and let the arrow fly. It landed slightly below the red silk. I turned to see Christian nodding. "Not quite enough, but still better than yesterday."

Christian's mother had been a friend of Lady Valerie's, and he was only a year older than I, so it happened that we'd become friends during my brief time at Queen Mary's court. As such, Lady Valerie had asked Christian to accompany us to Grayson Manor, and had then offered him the use of her son's vacant suite of rooms for the summer. His archery lessons were the product of his having happened upon me attempting to teach myself with borrowed bow and arrows.

"What is *enough* in archery?" I asked, nocking another arrow.

"It depends," he said, and I heard the smile in his voice.

"On what?" I drew the bowstring back to my cheek, feeling muscles I hadn't had two months ago tighten with the effort.

"On what you intend to kill," he said.

I flinched and my arrow flew impossibly wide. "Given the option," I said quietly, "I'd prefer not to kill."

His voice suddenly took on a concerned tone. "I was jesting. Of course you've no need to kill anything. As long as I am here to hunt for you, you and Lady Valerie shall always have meat to eat."

I turned to face him, one hand on my hip. "Whether or not I eat meat has nothing to do with my desire to learn archery."

"For sport then?" Christian's concern seemed to grow. "You can't mean to use it against a foe."

He was probably right, though in all honesty, learning to shoot an arrow had seemed a useful skill to add to the set Ringo, Saira, and Archer possessed.

But I could see that Christian needed my interest in archery to make sense. "Of course, for sport," I said lightly. "And I can't win with *good enough*, can I?"

Christian had turned every one of my lessons into a competition, and the sibling-like rivalry we'd developed reminded me a bit of the way Ringo and Saira were friends. It had been a revelation which had made me feel quite foolish for my small jealousies.

He grinned, apparently relieved at my answer. "Not against me you can't."

I returned my attention to the target and narrowed my focus to the bit of red silk, the whisper of a breeze in the leaves, and the beating of my own heart. I drew the bowstring back to my cheek, adjusted my aim, and let go. That arrow struck just left of the center of the target, and as I turned to gloat, I spotted Lady Valerie coming down the path.

"Ah, there you are, Charlotte." Lady Valerie sounded pleased to see me, but slightly less so to see Christian. "And you, too, Christian." I wondered at the change in her tone. Christian's grandmother had been Queen Catherine's lady of the bedchamber, and his grandfather had been a Moorish archer whose great skill and reputation as a weapons-maker to the old King Henry had elevated the status of his whole family. He certainly had more rank and status than I had, unless that was the problem?

"Well done on your shot, Miss Charlotte," Christian said formally as he stepped forward with his own bow and arrow. He aimed at the square of silk, and with a smooth, practiced motion, sent the arrow into the heart of red.

"Christian, your aim and skill surpass even my Henry's." Lady Valerie said in a tone that was at once as wistful as it was complimentary.

I wondered if the flattery was deliberate after the cool tone of her greeting. I turned to her with a smile. "He's a good teacher, and he makes excellent arrows."

She looked over at him, then back at me with a wry expression at my choice of garments. "You look very much as you did when I first met you in France," she said quietly as Christian busied himself out of earshot, collecting arrows.

I glanced at the heap of velvet on the grass and sighed. "I apologize to you, and I'll apologize to Meg after I've brushed the grass and dirt off the dress. It's just too hot and restricting to wear on such a lovely day when there are targets to shoot."

Lady Valerie laughed, and I was relieved that I hadn't disappointed her. At least not much.

"I'm happy to see the time at court didn't drum all the play out of you, and yet it is time to re-dress in the garments of a lady for your art lesson." She seemed to study me as I picked up the heavy gown. "The months *have* changed you, my dear."

"Well, I've gotten stronger," I said as lifted the dress over my head and Lady Valerie helped me lace it. Christian strode away with our bows and arrows as if he was more embarrassed to see me dress than he'd been at my hose and tunic.

"It's more than that," Lady Valerie said, as she tugged the laces tight. I was not a large person, and yet somehow the corsets could always make me gasp for air. "You've become someone accomplished." She took my arm, and we started down the path to the manor house.

"I feel changed," I said to her as we walked, "almost as though my real life is a dream I once had, or a story in a book."

"Your real life," she echoed quietly, and my conscience twinged, though I made an effort to square my shoulders as she'd taught me to do. I didn't apologize for the words I'd chosen, and I counted it a victory – proof that her lessons about being a lady of confidence and quality had sunken in.

"Do you miss the life you had before?" she asked.

I met her eyes. "I miss Ringo like I'd miss the sun if I couldn't feel it. But that's not the same as missing my life, is it?"

The path we took through the woods was dappled with sunlight and just wide enough for two. I wondered if the Grayson estate still existed in my time, and if so, would I ever be able to walk this same path arm-in-arm with Ringo.

Lady Valerie was silent for long enough that I asked, "Is everything all right?"

She exhaled and squeezed my arm. "Of course it is, I have you with me." She smiled at me as we mounted the steps to the manor house. "But now I have to relinquish you to Master Doran, who waits for you in the studio. And perhaps when you're finished painting with him you'll come to my rooms to tell me of your day?"

"I look forward to it," I said, as I kissed her cheek and left her in the main hall. Any time I could spend alone with Lady Valerie was the highlight of every day since we'd left Whitehall Palace and Queen Mary's court. The hours we spent with embroidery and sewing, or reading books from the manor's impressive library, or even the times we spent cutting and arranging flowers were precious to me.

I found Master Doran in the conservatory, which Lady Valerie had set up as an art studio when she'd hired the master painter to teach me. I'd only worked with Master Doran twice before, and a maid had been assigned to sit in the room with us each time. This time, however, Master Doran was already working on a sketch and Meg was nowhere to be seen.

"Shall I fetch my maid?" I asked him, as I entered the south-facing room, with whitewashed walls and large mullioned-glass windows.

"If you like," he said, looking up. "Or you can leave the door open. I'm no danger to your reputation."

"Are you not?" I asked, aware that my question was inappropriate even as I asked it. The tone of censure in Lady Valerie's voice at finding me alone with Christian had worked its way under my skin and made me testy, then I flushed with my own audacity. "Forgive me," I said, "and please do not answer."

There was laughter in Master Doran's eyes as he studied me. "The time in the country appears to suit you, Miss Kelly," he said. "And in answer to your question, I am no danger to you or your reputation because my affections are otherwise engaged, and your guardian knows me to be a man of honor."

I blushed at the warmth in his voice when he said 'affections' and busied myself with my pencils to cover my reaction. I wasn't certain whether it was his easy admission of love or something else that made me trust him, yet I didn't meet his eyes until he asked, "Will you show me what you've drawn this week?"

"I haven't left the estate," I said shyly, "so my sketch pad is full of my own fanciful notions."

"Show me the ones you're most proud of," he said gently. Master Doran was a young man still, though closer to Lady Valerie's age than my own, but his patience was that of someone who had lived a long time. It made him easy company, and I was pleased that my guardian had thought to add art lessons to the list of opportunities she insisted I have.

I turned the pages of my loose-leaf folder until I found a drawing I'd done of Cook and her kitchen staff baking desserts for an obligatory dinner party Lady Valerie had given for the vicar and his wife the week before.

Cook was a cheerful woman, full of all the best curves, including the perpetual smile on her lovely round face. She also had the spirit of a Dominia – a kind of entity that protected home and hearth – which had probably surrounded the cooks of Grayson Manor since it was first built. I'd tried to depict the warm gleam of light that surrounded her, which I doubted was visible to anyone without my *Other*-sight.

Master Doran studied the drawing for what seemed an especially long time. His eyes lingered on Cook, and a smile seemed to tug at the corners of his mouth as he took in her laughing face. My fingers itched to draw his expressive eyebrows and the curve of his own smile.

"I assume this lovely woman works here, at Grayson Manor?" he finally asked.

I smiled. "Cook very graciously allows me to sit in a corner of her kitchen, as long as I stay out of the danger zone of the food and the fire."

"But why did you say your drawings were fanciful notions? I think you've drawn the very essence of a satisfied Dominia, and I don't think even I could have done better. Show me others."

I stared at Master Doran, so surprised that I temporarily lost control of my tongue. "You can see ... her?"

He gave a very un-teacher-like shrug. "If you mean, do I see her true nature? I likely would if I were to sit in her kitchen. But you can draw her as she truly is. I'd say that takes a bit more skill than merely seeing through the face she shows the world."

Wordlessly, and with more instinct than conscious thought, I handed my art teacher the entire folder. He turned the pages carefully, holding the drawings by the edges so as not to smudge the pencil. The landscapes of the manor and the estate grounds received his technical notes on light and depth, and he set two of them aside to use as templates for paintings on canvas. But it was the drawings of the people who lived on the estate that seemed to capture his imagination. He asked questions about them, what their names were, how they fared, the substance of their work for Lady Valerie. It was their stories that interested him most, and he seemed pleased by my insight into the all the people I drew.

A few of those people were *Others* —he identified the boot boy as Fae and the head groom as a descendant of long-ago Centaurs. It was only when he got to the bottom of the stack, to the drawings I'd made of Christian both during our journey from court and after we'd arrived at the manor when I'd come across him crafting the arrows he'd made for me, that he studied them in silence.

Finally, he met my eyes again. "Does she know?"

My heart, which had seemed to skip a beat at the scrutiny he gave the drawings, raced. "Does Lady Valerie know that the ghost of her dead son, Henry, has attached himself to Christian de Cardenas?"

His eyebrow rose. "The ghost was her son?"

The air felt thick, and I nodded in silence.

"You knew him?"

"I was there when he died. It's—" the sound caught in my throat and I took a deep breath and tried again. "It's why I'm here, why she invited me to come."

He frowned and returned his gaze to the drawings. They were of Christian, but I'd overlayed his face with the echo of Henry's. Their features were similar enough that it looked like a blur or a mistake, but I saw the two different young men clearly. So, apparently, did my painting master.

"Has she seen these?" he asked, finally returning them to the folder.

I shook my head. "It's not the sort of thing she needs to hear from me – or anyone, really. It's only been a few months since he died, and she took it very hard."

"How much do you think she knows?" he asked. I heard concern in his voice, and curiosity.

"I don't believe it's something she's able to see herself," I said. "Whether she has the sense of his presence, I don't know. She seems attached to Christian, yet oddly uncomfortable when he's near."

Master Doran closed the folder and pushed it across the table to me. "It's a heavy burden you carry alone, Miss Kelly. I don't envy you the weight of it."

I exhaled. "Call me Charlotte, or Charlie if you prefer. Miss Kelly feels too formal for someone who holds my secrets."

He smiled gently. "Miss Charlotte, owning the truth is powerful, and the only discovery that should be feared is the discovery of lies."

I regarded him steadily. He had a manner that spoke of his own considerable power, and yet he was in the country teaching art techniques to the ward of a retired lady-in-waiting to an aging queen.

"How do you know Lady Valerie?" I finally asked him.

"I introduced myself to her at court," he said finally.

"Why?"

His smile was genuine and friendly, and so much more honest than that of any courtier I'd met in my time at Whitehall. "Because I thought you might want a teacher," he said, "and because there may come a time when you've learned what you set out to learn, and you need a way home."

My heart beat so loudly in my ears I thought he could hear it. Was he a Clocker? Could he take me back to Ringo if I asked him to? But before I could ask one of the many questions that pelted around my brain, he continued.

"That time is not today, however, as there any many more things to learn, and perhaps one or two to teach as well."

And then he brought forward a blank canvas and taught me how to prepare it for paint.

I found Lady Valerie in the private sitting room attached to her bedroom suite. She sat by the window, the embroidery hoop forgotten in her lap as she looked out at the view. She hadn't heard me come in and only realized I was there when I came over to see what so fascinated her.

"Oh, Charlotte. You startled me. I was just woolgathering." She gestured vaguely at her embroidery as I stepped closer to the window.

"Christian is very accomplished with the bow," I said, looking down at the young man who had set up his own target practice in the hedge maze and was currently running through it, shooting at each silk-tied branch he encountered.

She sighed softly. "My Henry was much the same. Always making a game of every task and challenging himself to be faster, stronger, better. He, too, was quite adept at the bow."

She finally met my eyes. "You may have wondered at a shift in my mood this morning when I came upon the two of you in the woods."

"I admit I did notice," I said softly.

"When I invited Christian to accompany us from London, I thought that perhaps the tentative friendship you'd struck with him could, with time and proximity, become something more."

I opened my mouth to protest, but she held up a hand. "Let me finish, please, my dear. I do know how you feel about your Ringo — or at least how you felt about him when I brought you here."

I ignored every bit of my training and interrupted Lady Valerie before she could say more. "I love Ringo and will go back to him if he'll have me. I am here with you now, and there's no place I'd rather be, but I want to be very clear that he is my future. I choose him and always will."

Her eyes filled with tears, and she inhaled sharply. "I hoped that perhaps you'd find a reason to stay here and allow me the smallest taste of what it was to be a mother again." She seemed to grope for the words she still had left to say. "Motherhood died for me with my son, and it was unfair of me to pin such hopes on you. When I saw you today, in virtually your underclothes, I realized just how reckless I'd been to think Christian could tempt you."

I knelt beside her chair and took her hands in mine. "First, Christian and I are friends. I trust him, and you should know he'd never betray you. And second," I said, pausing to catch her gaze with mine, "you will never stop being a mother to a dead son." Tears welled in her eyes, but I continued to hold her hands. "And I will never stop being the daughter and sister of dead women. But even as their deaths shaped us, they need not define us. You are not only mother to Henry, you mother me, and even Christian. And I can be daughter to you and sister to Saira without diminishing the importance of the mother and sister I had before I met you."

She lifted my hand to her mouth and kissed it as the sound of Christian's cry of *whoop!* drew our eyes outside to the center of the maze where he hopped around in a circle with his bow brandished above his head like a trophy.

"He's so like my Henry sometimes," she murmured, as though lost in thought.

"Sometimes," I began hesitantly, "the spirits of our loved ones might linger around us in more than our memories. Perhaps that is the case with Henry." I breathed in quietly, careful to keep my voice even and calm.

She continued to watch Christian through the window, and something in her expression seemed to soften. But then Lady Valerie shook her head, as if to clear the image from her mind. I wondered if she had denied the validity of my words, or if she had accepted my vague truth as possible.

But finally, the dreamy sadness in Lady Valerie's eyes cleared, and she met my gaze with an intensity that surprised me. "I love you, Charlotte Kelly, and I will love you no matter where you go, no matter who you love, and no matter what you choose. I hope that when Saira comes for you – and I'm certain she will if she can – you choose the future that makes you *whoop* with joy."

A memory of Ringo's laughter filled my mind, and I smiled with my whole heart. "I already have."

Cheating Death – A Summary

Ringo, Saira, and Archer traveled back in time to ask Charlie for help with their plan to defeat the Mongers' grab for power over the Immortal Descendants. Ringo explained to her that he had two questions, but he'd ask the most important one only after they had dealt with the Mongers. Charlie jumped at the chance to join her friends, making sure Saira promised to eventually take her back to the moment right after she left 1554 so she could explain everything to Lady Valerie without worrying her.

The battle itself is way too cool to summarize here, so if you want a reminder of how The Immortal Descendants series wrapped up, I recommend a re-read. But after everyone got back to the business of living their lives, Saira took us to a very special event for Ringo and Charlie. I invite you to re-experience it here as the story of their life together begins…

CHEATING DEATH – THE WEDDING

GRAYSON MANOR – 1554

The manor house was draped in mistletoe, fir, and yew for Christmas, and lovely decorations of dried oranges and holly wreaths filled the rooms. Archer and I were given a guest room usually reserved for visiting royalty, which, according to Valerie Grayson, we were.

I joined Valerie and my mom in Charlie's bedroom, where a maid was lifting a stunning gold dress over Charlie's linen shift. Valerie dismissed the maid and fastened the dress up herself.

"Oh Charlie, you look so beautiful," my mom exclaimed. She had tears in her eyes when she looked up at me, and I was so glad she had come with us to this wedding, especially since she had missed mine.

Charlie caught my eyes. "I seriously considered searching the Elian Manor closets for something to wear from the 1950s, but it takes a certain degree of fortitude to wear these gowns, and I felt that perhaps I was finally strong enough."

I took her hands in mine, and the diamond band Ringo had made for her sparkled like stars on her finger. "Charlie, you were strong enough the day I met you. The only difference now is that you actually believe it."

Valerie had finished fastening the exquisitely embroidered gown. She studied the young woman she had helped shape, and her gaze filled with tenderness. "My dear, the time you gave me has been the most precious gift I've ever received. Thank you for allowing me to dote on you, and to love you as my own daughter."

She kissed both of Charlie's cheeks, and there were definitely tears in her eyes when she looked away.

"Why is it that weddings make people cry?" Charlie whispered to me as my mom and Valerie sorted through Valerie's jewelry cases for sparkly things to drape on the bride.

I shrugged. "I have theories, but it's more fun to make something up."

She grinned. "Oh do!"

"I think people don't *fall* in love, but instead, love starts as a tiny butterfly, usually in the belly, because that's where we feel it first. And that butterfly multiplies and multiplies, until our whole being is filled with the butterflies of being in love. Then, at a wedding when two people declare and promise that love out loud, the room fills with their butterflies, and people cry with the beauty of it."

"Oh, I like that story! Today, if I feel nervous, I'll imagine the whole room full of butterflies."

I smiled at my beautiful friend who was in love with the brother of my heart. "It will be."

Ringo and Charlie's wedding was intimate and lavish. He and Archer both wore gentlemen's suits from 1889, and mom and I were in Tudor gowns, borrowed from Valerie and quickly altered by her dressmaker. Millicent and mom had thrown them a wonderful engagement party at Elian Manor before we left, but Millicent had declined to Clock with us. We didn't press the issue.

Ringo's eyes shone as he promised to love, honor, and cherish Charlie all the days of their lives, and when Charlie's eyes filled with tears, she looked at me and we both looked up at all the imaginary butterflies that filled the hall.

When I hugged Ringo after the ceremony, I whispered to him, "I'm glad you finally asked her that first question."

He looked at me with the eyes of a man. "I'm glad I loved you first – it gave me a foundation to build on. I just never imagined how high it could go until I saw her again."

"She's a very lucky girl," I said with my whole heart, and then I replayed his words in my head with surprise. "You've lost your accent."

An impish grin lit up his face. "It let me blend in on the streets, but now I have a fine wife, and she deserves a proper gentleman."

The feast afterwards in the candlelit dining hall was fit for a king, but because it was just us, we moved a small table near the fireplace and sat together like a family, telling stories and laughing until late in the night.

Valerie gave the couple her wedding present first. "I've bought a property near Marylebone Park in London. I intend to build a townhouse there, and I will set up a trust that names you, Charlotte, as my heir. As I fear things may become tangled during the next three hundred years, I would like to name Lord Archer Devereux as the executor for the title of the property until such time as Charlotte and her husband can claim it. I'm sure the solicitors in the 19th century will be able to find you, Archer."

Charlie jumped up and hugged Valerie, which was no mean feat in all the heavy fabric of her dress, Ringo kissed the back of Valerie's hand, and Archer bowed. "It would be my pleasure, madam."

They had a home, and the excitement that shone on Charlie's face was palpable. My mom stood up and brought a small wrapped package to Charlie, who was clearly in on whatever was inside that box, because she turned and gave it to Valerie.

"My wedding gift to Charlotte is not one that she has the ability to use. You do, however, and I trust that my daughter can teach you the finer points."

Valerie looked confused until she opened the box. Inside, on a bed of dark blue velvet, lay the Clocker necklace. Valerie gasped and looked up at her foster daughter with shining eyes. "I'll be able to visit you?" she asked.

"I can teach you how to focus your travel so that you clock to their house on a certain date. It means you're probably going to have to build a walled garden at the house so we can put a spiral in it." I said.

"Oh!" Valerie's voice was choked with tears and she clapped her hands together in delight. "I might one day see my grandchildren!" She flung her arms around Charlie and Ringo first, and then my mom and me. "It will of course be handed back to the Elian line after I'm gone." And then, just for good measure, she kissed Archer on the cheek. There was happy crying all the way around the table, and it took several handkerchiefs and some manly throat-clearing to get ourselves under control.

"And now, from Saira and myself …" Archer pulled two envelopes out of the inside pocket of his dinner jacket and handed them to Ringo, who held Archer's gaze a long time before he finally opened the first one. His hand shook very slightly as he passed the letter to Charlie, whose gasp at the first line caused Valerie to slide her chair next to Charlie to read over her shoulder. Ringo stood up and came to our side of the table.

He held a hand out to help me up from my chair. "My lady …" His voice choked. "Thank you," he finally managed to whisper. I held his face and kissed him on both cheeks.

"You're welcome."

Ringo embraced Archer in the kind of hug I'd only seen them do one other time – the first time they met again after Archer's infection. It was the grip of brothers, and their eyes were shiny when they parted.

Valerie's voice rose in confusion. "Please excuse my ignorance of modern banking. There is an account set up for Mr. and Mrs. Ringo Devereux at Rothschild & Sons? But that is your name, is it not, Archer?"

"It is my brother's name too," he said with a grin at Ringo. "Open the other one."

"I'm not sure I can," Ringo said, wiping away the tears.

I laughed. "Charlie, Ringo has butterflies in his eyes. Could you do it, please?"

She giggled and slit open the second envelope. This time her gasp was even louder. "Oh, Ringo! It's an admission from King's College London for Ringo Devereux, to study the discipline of his choice, and for Charlotte Devereux to the Ladies Department of King's College for the same."

Ringo stared at Archer open-mouthed. "But King's is for the upper classes."

Archer smirked. "You carry a Lord's name and bank statement. I think you qualify."

There was another round of embraces and some more tears before we all returned to our seats.

"By the way, we've arranged with the modern Rothschild bank to call us any time a letter appears in a certain safety deposit box. You'll have to give us a day or two notice — at least long enough for them to do their daily box-check — but the system should work okay for arranging visits." I had been so happy when Archer told me what he had in mind, based on the way Tom had left us a message. I had actually gone back to 1945 to test it with the Rothschild banker I knew, and it had worked perfectly.

It was the only thing that was going to make saying goodbye tolerable. Our days with Ringo and Charlie had been too brief, and although they did consider staying in our time permanently, they realized they actually did want to experience getting older day by day, instead of all at once with a visit back.

So they were our constant companions during the two months after the Monger battle. They sat in on Council meetings that were open to all Descendants, and experienced the shaping of Descendant politics first-hand. They divided their time between Elian Manor and rooms in the newly opened wings at St. Brigid's, where mixed-blood Descendants were now eligible to send their children to school. Charlie studied botany with Mr. Shaw, and managed to teach him some of the old plant lore she had learned during her time at Grayson Manor. And when he wasn't with us, Ringo spent every minute with Connor, either in the laboratory or playing video games and tinkering with electronic gadgets.

We took Ringo and Charlie with us the first time we visited the house in Galway that Millicent gave us. That had been a working trip spent cleaning and repairing the beautiful old place on the Cliffs of Moher. Ringo was the one who pointed out that a scene from *The Princess Bride* had been filmed at those cliffs, and our running joke of the weekend became answering "as you wish" to any request.

Ringo's friendship with Tom had also deepened. Ringo understood Tom in ways even Adam didn't, and it was Ringo who was able to convince Tom to accept the position as Monger Head on the Descendants' Council. There were full-blooded Mongers from the Rothchild/Walters regime who objected, but when Raven and the soldiers who had fought in the Monger battle stood up for Tom, the dissention quieted to a low murmur.

Probably the most karmic ending of all belonged to Seth Walters, who died from blood poisoning. He had believed until the end that Archer was a Vampire, and had injected Archer's Seer blood into his Monger veins. He was dead for three days before anyone found him.

The engagement party that Millicent and my mom threw for Ringo and Charlie had also been a going away party, and I'd never felt so much love and friendship in one room. My mom confided in me that night that Mr. Shaw had asked her to marry him. He was the new Shifter Head, and I had returned the Shifter bone into his safekeeping. They felt they needed to bring the matter before the Council, but they weren't asking for permission or forgiveness, just acceptance.

After we left Grayson Manor, I took Archer back to modern St. Brigid's before Clocking Ringo and Charlie to 1889. Archer couldn't return to Victorian London because he was already there – and already a Vampire. Except things had changed now, and Archer from 1889 found us at the Baker Street townhouse that Valerie had built for Charlie and Ringo. My mom had gone to Elian Manor to see her sister, so it was just the four of us.

"How much do you want to know, Archer?" I asked him, when we were seated in the library across from Ringo and Charlie.

He smiled at me, and it was my Archer exactly. They all were – every version of him, from every age – he was *my* Archer. "All of it has changed already, hasn't it? This life that I will live is already different than the one I did live because you have changed it."

"It's not a time stream split though, because the only person really affected is you." I said. "I think it's more of a time stream overlay. Whatever happens to you as you move forward in time won't change the fact of what did happen. It all just lays over the top, so that as you experience things now, you'll remember them in my time as well."

"There are differences though," he said quietly as he looked down at the crowned heart ring on my left hand.

I smiled and held the hand out to him. "There are, but we can work around them."

A House Called Home

London – 1889

"We're home." Maybe it was wonder, or relief, or possibly trepidation that made the words come out on a breath. When Charlie met my eyes I saw the same wonder, or relief, or possibly trepidation in her expression.

We stared around us at the enormous entry hall of the townhouse Lady Valerie had left to Charlie in her will. The house had been built to the specifications she left with trustees, and then leased to tenants throughout the years to pay for its own upkeep, but it had stood empty for the past year waiting for us to arrive.

Under Archer's stewardship the kitchen and upstairs lavatories had been modernized with the latest Victorian technology, and comfortable furnishings had been procured for the public rooms that we'd seen. We'd been so intent on building a fire in the library and spending precious time with Saira and Archer when we'd arrived earlier in the day that we hadn't even toured the huge place. But now that Saira and Archer had gone — she, through the spiral portal in the garden back to the 21ˢᵗ century, and he — well, I wasn't exactly sure where he'd gone after Saira left. If I had to guess, I'd say he went somewhere cold and dreary to miss her. It's what I would have done in his place.

But I wasn't in his place. I was in my place. Our place. I stood in an entry hall three times the size of the hidden flat I'd once shared with the woman who was now my wife, and the words I'd just uttered in wonder and trepidation felt oddly and inescapably right because she was at my side.

This house, however, threatened to upend that feeling.

It had gotten dark early, and the double-height entry hall was nearly as frigid as the winter outside. There were shadows in the formal dining room beyond the hall that threatened to creep out in search of someone to haunt, and I felt Charlie shiver beside me.

Her eyes found mine again. "Should we look for a place to sleep, or go back to the warmth of the fire?"

My feet were already moving us toward the library. "Fire. Definitely."

I fed the flames with wood and then settled back into the velvet sofa we'd moved in front of the fireplace. Charlie snuggled into my side and draped a wool shawl over both of us.

She sighed. "This doesn't feel real."

I squeezed her closer to me. "*This* does," I said, feeling her smile against my chest.

She looked up at me. "Shouldn't we …" Her voice trailed off, and the trepidation was back in her eyes. She took a deep, bracing breath. "It's our first night together in our new home – our first night together alone as husband and wife. Aren't there rules about beds and such?"

I chuckled, and felt her relax against me again. "I'm not much of a rule follower, and I am perfectly content to sit here tonight, next to this fire, with the woman I love in my arms." There was time – a lifetime, in fact – to learn the things about each other that we would learn, and I was determined to appreciate every moment of the journey. The day had been exciting, emotional, and long, and I felt remarkably like a cat lounging by the fire, unable and unwilling to move.

She snuggled in again with her head on my chest, and I kissed her hair. "Oh good," she said. "I have the feeling the house will require daylight to explore properly, and for now, I'm happiest right here."

"Despite the chill, the silence, and the far-too-large house," I said, drawing my wife close to my side, "when you're in my arms, I am home."

"Get out!" a voice shrieked just before a pillow hit my head. "Get out you filthy vagrants. Get out!" Another blow with the pillow just missed me as I surged to my feet to face our attacker. It was a woman of indeterminate age, with graying hair and a fierce expression, wearing a coat and hat dusted with snow.

I blinked in surprise to realize that Charlie and I had fallen asleep on the library sofa. She, too, had leapt to her feet to avoid the woman's pillow attack, and recovered faster than I. "Good morning, madam.

May we help you?" Charlie's voice was remarkably serene in the face of the shrieking, pillow-wielding woman.

"I don't know what you think ye're about, sleeping in someone else's house, but you'll get out now before I call the constables." The woman's volume had diminished slightly, but her ferocity had not.

"*We* are the owners of this house," I said, finally finding my own voice. "And who might you be?"

The woman snorted in disbelief. "No you're not. You're too young, for one thing. Mr. and Mrs. Devereux are respectable people with money." She looked us up and down with disdain. "Something you're clearly not."

Her disdain ignited something in my blood, and I took a step forward. The woman must have seen something on my face, because her eyes widened slightly. She held her ground though, and I spoke in my deepest voice to shake her confidence.

"Madam, I can see by your clothing that you live in Houndsditch, and that the rag fair market trade has declined for you with the winter. I assume, based on the timing of your arrival and the fact that you appear to have a key to our home, that you were scheduled to come prepare the house yesterday, before our return to London. Since the snow made travel difficult for you, you assumed we, too, would be delayed a day. I imagine the omnibus trip you took to get here this morning was cold and uncomfortable, and I will give you the fare for a private carriage and see that your wages for the day are paid if you give me the key and the name of the firm which contracted you."

Her mouth had fallen open with my opening observation, and then snapped shut with my request for the house key. "Now see here——" she began furiously.

Charlie stepped forward before I could, and she propelled the woman out of the room. "Come," she said. "We only arrived last night, and I have yet to find the kitchen. Perhaps we can find it together, Mrs...?"

"Mrs. Morris," the woman said begrudgingly.

I let them go on ahead, disappointed that the first day of our new lives together had begun so loudly. I suppose I should have anticipated that someone came occasionally to clean, as the house didn't feel or look as though it had been closed up for months. I sighed and went to work rebuilding the fire in the library to ward off the chill of the snowy morning.

Twenty minutes later, as I was about to go searching the house for my wife, she came in bearing a tray. "I sent Mrs. Morris home with a week's pay and was able to retrieve this," she said as she set the tray on the library table and fished a key from her pocket. "She won't be returning, and if we write to the firm of Burns and Paulson, no one else will be either."

I pulled Charlie into my arms and breathed easier for her presence there. "Thank you. You are magic."

She laughed softly, and the sound lightened my spirits. "Yes, I am. Though the menace in your tone certainly helped. Wherever did you find that voice?"

"There was a small man who worked at the docks where Gosford ran his boat. He used to bellow to the captains when it was their turn to come in, and his voice could cut through the fog on the river like a foghorn. His normal speaking voice was nothing remarkable, and I asked him once how he did it. The man, his name was Kumar, said the trick was to find the giant inside yourself and let him speak."

"There's a giant inside you?" Charlie said with a smile as she added two sugars and a dollop of cream to the tea she'd poured for me. I preferred coffee, but I would have to devise a way to brew it the way I liked it.

"There is," I said, accepting the tea with a smile. "The giant has this massive heart, full of love for his wife, and he developed a—" I dropped my voice down low "—really big voice to tell her about it."

She laughed. "I prefer your normal voice to that menace, if it's all the same to you. Though I do appreciate its purpose." She sipped her tea for a moment as she studied the fire.

"It was a truly awful way to wake up, wasn't it?" I said ruefully.

"The worst, I think, was being told we're not—" she waved her hand around airily "—enough to live here." Then she took a deep, fortifying breath. "Well, I suppose we shall have to be grown-ups and explore the house."

"I'm not sure I want to be grown up," I said, "because if we're not playing hide and seek while we do it, are we really exploring?"

My wife's slow smile was a beautiful thing to behold as she placed her tea cup on the tray and reached up to kiss my cheek before she bolted from the room.

Playing hide and seek in a five-bedroom townhome with enough space for six full-time staff was an excellent way to explore our new domicile. The large main hall included a grand staircase that ascended to a level where we found two formal drawing rooms with separate studies, plus the five bedrooms, and another staircase leading to the servants' quarters and box rooms. In the basement were rooms including a housekeeper's bedroom, a laundry, a larder, a wine cellar, and others with various purposes for which we could only guess. On the ground floor, to the right of the main hall, was the library, a study, the dining room, and a remarkably progressive kitchen. To the left of the main hall was another, more masculine study, a rather floral sitting room, and, unbelievably, a ballroom.

The rooms to which we gravitated were the library and the kitchen. The first study seemed like a good overflow library, and the study across the entry hall was full of dark and heavy furniture. The floral sitting room felt too fancy to relax in, and shadows made the dining room one to avoid. The ballroom had potential as a place to practice archery and sword fighting, and worked well as a skating rink for our stockinged feet. But none of the second floor bedrooms felt like a place in which we'd feel comfortable sleeping. The large four-poster beds were too imposing, and there was virtually no other furniture in them to make them comfortable. The single lavatory on the floor, though advanced for its time, couldn't compete with the bathtub we'd had in the middle of the kitchen in my hidden flat.

"Which room, besides the library and the kitchen, is your favorite?" I asked Charlie after I found her behind the curtains in a second floor drawing room.

"This one," she said, turning toward the view of Regent's Park out the window. She inhaled as if drawing the cold air outside into her lungs. "I could watch the dogs and children play all day."

Two large puppies, one black and sleek, and one dust-colored and shaggy were cavorting in the snow in the park across the drive from us. I chuckled at their antics. "We should make this our bedroom," I said.

"Can we do that?" Charlie asked as she looked out at the view. "Aren't visitors supposed to be received in formal drawing rooms?"

I wrapped my arms around her waist. "Yes, we can do that. We can do anything. It's our house."

She leaned her head back onto my shoulder. "You say that, and yet I still feel as though that awful woman is shrieking, 'Get out! You don't belong here!' And truly, I don't belong. I don't feel old enough, or wealthy enough, or substantial enough to even be a guest in a house with a ballroom, much less to own one."

"You lived in the Grayson Estate for nearly a year, and it was much bigger than this."

"Grayson Estate was in the country, and seeing the stars every night reminded me that you were in the world with those same stars overhead. That has nothing to do with a ballroom."

"It could," I said mischievously, and she poked me in the ribs.

"Your flat above the accountancy office felt like home. Maybe we can recreate that in the ballroom," she said with a snort that made me laugh. "You think I'm joking," she said with a mock pout.

"I know exactly what you mean," I said. Her words echoed my own thoughts to the degree that I turned her around to face me. "Let's go there," I said. "Let's take a bath in our ridiculous bathtub and contemplate why we like that flat. Who knows?" I shrugged. "We may decide to live there after all."

It felt like a lifetime since I'd been to my flat, and longer since Charlie and I had been there together. And even though very little had changed about the place, everything had changed for us, and I was suddenly aware how intimate it was.

Charlie kicked off her shoes at the top of the stairs, as usual, and walked around the attic space touching her small drawings and trailing fingers across the big chair in which she'd slept for so many months. Her small potted herbs had long-since dried, and she crumbled the rosemary between her fingers, releasing the savory scent into the frigid room.

It was a Sunday, which had been the one day a week that we'd been able to move freely during the daylight hours. I lit the small gas stove that heated the water for the bathtub, put the kettle on for tea, and readied the teapot.

Charlie finally sat at the table across from me. "I never realized how careful I've always been," she said.

I frowned as I poured the hot water into the teapot. "What do you mean?"

She gestured around the attic. "Well, first of all, we had to be completely silent during the days when the accountants worked, and all of our entrances and exits had to be timed for when they wouldn't be downstairs."

I nodded as I filled our mugs. "I guess that's just how it always was, so I didn't really consider it a difficulty."

She wrapped her hands around her mug to warm them. "And second, this was your flat, your space. I never wanted to take up your room here or change anything that you did. Even putting my drawings up on the walls felt like I was encroaching."

"I love your drawings, Charlie. I loved coming home to find a new scene from the market or something you'd sketched for a story," I said quietly, trying to understand the reserve I saw in her.

She finally met my eyes and whispered, "I was terrified you'd see how much I loved you and you'd ask me to leave. It's why I left first and went with Lady Valerie."

My chest tightened at the worry in her face. "I don't understand. Why would I want you to leave? I loved you. I love you," I corrected.

She finally smiled, a quiet, sad smile, and picked up my hand to kiss it. "I know that now. But like that house in Marylebone, you were big and grand and certain of your place in the world, and I felt like a girl tiptoeing silently through life, too careful to understand that sliding around ballrooms in stockings is much more fun."

She stood then, put the plug in the bottom of the tub, then turned on the water. She added a little of the lemon rosemary oil she'd made a lifetime before, and then she turned to meet my eyes. "I'm done being careful, Ringo. I will not love you carefully." She lifted the edge of her skirts and tugged off her stockings one by one. "I will love you with abandon and joy." She unbuttoned the front of her dress, holding my gaze with her own. "I will play games with you, and run, and laugh, and dance, and I will trust you with my heart," she said, dropping her dress off her shoulders, "my body," she stepped out of her skirt and stood, shivering in just a thin linen chemise, "and my soul."

I broke free from the paralysis that transfixed me and went to her, wrapping her in my arms and kissing her with the whole of my being. And when the bath was full enough for two, the only care we took was not to splash too much water on the floor.

Charlie's drawings replaced the pen and ink prints in the library, and we spent a day moving the furniture on the second floor until we had designed a bedroom that felt as intimate as our hidden flat. We turned the other drawing room into a guest room for Lady Valerie's eventual visits, and then distributed the rest of the drawing room furniture throughout the house. Meals were simple bread and soup affairs cooked together and eaten at the kitchen table, and evenings were spent quietly by the library fire.

We existed inside the bubble of our enormously quiet house, going for walks in the park, seeing no one but the shopkeepers, and staying entirely within the boundaries of Marylebone. About a week after our arrival at the house, as I sat at the kitchen table repairing a gas lamp and Charlie peeled potatoes for supper, a knock sounded at the kitchen door. My wife met my eyes in a silent question as I got up to open it.

A woman stood outside, busily shaking off an umbrella. She looked up as I appeared in the doorway. "I'm Mrs. Mac. You'll be expecting me from Burns and Paulson?" Her accent was thickly Scottish, her voice brusque, her manner no-nonsense, and her gaze direct. I stepped back automatically to let her in out of the rain.

"I'm sorry, I don't think we were expecting anyone," I said lamely.

Charlie wiped her hands on her apron and held one out to shake Mrs. Mac's. "Hello, I'm Charlotte Devereux, and this is my husband, Ringo. May we help you?"

Mrs. Mac seemed to take in every bit of our appearance and the scene in the kitchen in one sweeping glance. "If you weren't expecting me, you should've been," she said finally. "I believe you sent Mrs. Morris away, which, in my opinion, showed excellent judgment, however you've called for no replacement, and that is decidedly less wise. The two of you cannot run a house this size without help. Now, I'll do general housekeeping and some of the cooking, but I'll need a girl in twice a week to help with the cleaning, and if you have many guests, you'll need an errand boy as well."

Charlie and I were both as stunned by Mrs. Mac's pronouncements as by her presence.

"We don't generally have guests," Charlie finally said.

Mrs. Mac took off her coat and hat and hung them on a hook by the door. "Right, then. I'll need a room and a sitting room to myself, preferably belowstairs, and two half-days off a week to visit my sister. I expect sixty pound per year, but as I'm cooking for you as well, it's not an outrageous sum."

I finally found my tongue again. "We sent word to Burns and Paulson specifically declining any further staff. How did you really find us, Mrs. Mac?" I kept my tone mild, and Mrs. Mac didn't so much as flinch at being caught in the lie, which could have indicated anything from composure under pressure to having had significant practice at it.

Mrs. Mac narrowed her gaze at me. "Are you calling me a liar, Mr. Devereux?"

An interesting offensive tactic, and generally effective against much of polite society. As I had never had much patience with that particular society, I decided to see how far her composure under pressure extended. With a quick glance at Charlie to get her nodded permission, I studied the woman who stood in our kitchen.

"If this is, indeed, a job interview, Mrs. Mac, it is imperative that we know you in order that we may trust you, would you not agree?

"If you're disinclined to believe me, it doesn't matter what I say, does it?" Her tone was not defensive, but merely matter-of-fact, a distinction I found intriguing.

"Would you like me to tell you what I see?" I asked pleasantly.

The catch in her breath was barely perceptible, but to her credit, she tilted her head in acquiescence. "By all means, Mr. Devereux." Then, so as not to see my gaze on her, she tied on an apron and took the potato peeler out of Charlie's hand, shooing her to the table to sit. I observed her while she worked, peeling and slicing potatoes into thin chips.

Mrs. Mac was a handsome woman, tall and sturdy, with auburn hair pulled loosely back in a braided chignon. She looked to be in her thirties, with an unexpectedly full-lipped mouth that I had yet to see smile. Her clothing was well-fitted and made of a flattering blue-gray wool. The color and the small bit of lace at her throat softened the otherwise severe practicality of her well-made wardrobe. She looked, sounded, and seemed perfectly, respectably middle class.

"Well," I said, running through the list of my observations, "you are left-handed, obviously."

Mrs. Mac snorted, arched an eyebrow as if to say 'that's all you've got?' and held up the peeler, which she wielded with her left hand.

I smiled. "As determined from the callous on your left middle finger and the weave of your braided hair."

Mrs. Mac's mouth twitched, and she very nearly rolled her eyes. I found myself wanting to impress her.

"You were raised with means and given an education, as evidenced by your speech, but you left home when you were young to make your own way – hence the housekeeper position."

The eyebrow went up again, but she focused on slicing potatoes, so I couldn't see her expression. I dug a little deeper.

"You likely prefer walking to every other mode of transportation, which I can see in the care you take of your boots. And you're also a dab hand with a sewing needle and likely made your own clothes."

"Because her clothes are so lovely?" Charlie asked, intrigued. "Deduction" was a game Charlie and I sometimes played – I would make up stories about people based on the things I noticed, and she would attempt to guess what I'd seen.

I answered Charlie, determined to also impress my wife with my observations. "Because women's clothing traditionally buttons on the left, and her jacket and blouse button right, as men's do."

I attempted to mitigate the rudeness of speaking about a person who was in the room, by again addressing my observations to Mrs. Mac herself. "Either you're immensely practical and see no reason to conform to a practice built on the notion that women need help to dress themselves, or it's equally likely that you grew used to buttoning clothes that way when you were young, and have customized your adult clothing accordingly."

"But you said she was raised with means. Do you assume she had no help dressing?" Charlie asked. Too late I noticed Mrs. Mac's shoulders stiffen, and my mouth snapped shut as I considered the best way forward without causing more hurt than I inadvertently had done.

Mrs. Mac spoke before I could formulate an answer. "No, I assume he means that I began life dressing as a boy, at least for a time."

Charlie shrugged, "Oh, well, so did I."

Mrs. Mac looked so nonplussed that Charlie continued speaking. "I find dresses to be so much more enjoyable to wear, don't you, Mrs. Mac? It's very clever of you to customize your clothing for dressing yourself. I have to choose things that button in the front, or else ask Ringo for help."

I now thought I knew the source of her composure when caught in the lie, and hoped it was discretion, rather than ease with lying, that was at the heart of it.

"I …" Mrs. Mac began, then finally exhaled a breath she might have been holding for weeks, if the relief in her posture was any indication. "Thank you," she said to Charlie. Then her eyes darted to me, and seeing that my expression held no surprise or judgment, she spoke again.

"You are very observant, Mr. Devereux." I tilted my head in silent agreement, and she continued. "I am too. You asked how I knew to call here for work – well, I saw you."

"You … saw us?" There were so many possible interpretations of those words in a world where Descendants of Fate could See the future.

But perhaps it was as uncomplicated as it sounded, because she continued in the same no-nonsense tone she'd used when describing why we needed her. "You leave by the garden gate every morning to fetch fresh bread, and Mrs. Devereux goes for eggs and the odd vegetable in the afternoons. No one else comes to the front door or the back, indicating that you have no one to shop for you, no one to clean for you. So you're either squatting in this fine house, doing for yourselves in a place that requires more hands than you've got, or you're here legitimately and just have no idea how to go about hiring help. Either way, you need my skills, and I'm here to offer them."

She had heated fat on the cooker and was frying the sliced potatoes with an efficiency that was far cleaner than any attempt I'd ever made.

"Tell me, Mrs. Mac," I said, impressed at her own observational skills and wanting to make amends for my earlier insensitivity, "about the job you're leaving to work here."

She met my eyes with a quick, surprised glance before returning her attention to the potatoes. "There's naught to tell," she said. "I gave proper notice, and I've already been replaced – by Mrs. Morris, if you must know." Her lips thinned in what appeared to be disapproval, and I couldn't say I disagreed with the sentiment.

"May I ask at which number you worked?" I persisted, wanting to find the final piece to the puzzle. Why would anyone allow someone so obviously intelligent and capable to leave their employ?

A deep inhalation and the set of her jaw were the only indications she'd heard me until the potatoes were draining on a plate, the excess fat scooped from the pan, and eggs were frying in a pat of butter. When the eggs were plated and the pan moved off the flame, she turned to face me with a hand on one hip and an expression that dared me to comment. "If you must know, I worked at number four for three years. I was the housekeeper responsible for a staff of twelve, which swelled to twenty several times a month when the family entertained. My work was impeccable, and if you ask any of the staff I supervised, they'd say the same."

But not the homeowners at number four, I thought grimly. My tone remained conversational, however. "I recently met the lady of that house walking in the park with her adult daughter. Isn't it interesting that the most vocal proponents of the scriptures are often the least able to love their neighbors as themselves? Their views about how people should look and who they should be are rather … intolerant."

Mrs. Mac seemed to study me, and then she finally cleared her throat. "Indeed."

She added the crisps to the plates, included a sprig of parsley she'd found who knew where, and placed them in front of us on the table.

"Thank you, Mrs. Mac. This looks wonderful," Charlie said, with a beaming smile.

I tucked in, and indeed, the food was well-seasoned and perfectly cooked. When I'd taken appreciative bites, I looked up to see Mrs. Mac watching us eat with what seemed like a mixture of pride and concern.

I wiped my mouth and set down my fork and knife. "We are not … conventional," I began. "Charlie and I were not brought up to be gentry, our experiences have not fit expectations of normal, and it's quite likely they never will."

I met Charlie's eyes with a raised eyebrow, and she nodded her approval, so I continued. "Managing our household will likely require patience, a degree of fortitude, and certainly tolerance, but we promise the same in return. Mrs. Mac, would you be willing to work with us as a housekeeper, to cook for us occasionally, manage whatever staff you feel is necessary, and tolerate our differences? In return you shall have a full day, plus a half day off, private rooms belowstairs, paid medical care with the physician of your choice as needed, and one hundred pounds a year. Does that suit you?"

Only the barest hesitation betrayed her surprise. "It suits. I'll return tomorrow with my things." She removed her apron and hung it on the hook from which she took her hat and coat. When she'd replaced her outerwear and picked up her umbrella, she turned to us again. "Enjoy your supper," she said as she stepped out into the night.

She was back before the door had closed behind her. "If the two pups in your garden are to come inside, they'll need baths before they step foot on my kitchen floor." Her tone was stern, and we both started to our feet in surprise, but as she looked out the door, presumably at the dogs which had found their way into our garden, she smiled.

It was a lovely smile.

Mrs. Mac was gone before Charlie and I had our boots and coats on, and when we stepped out into the rain, the forms of two puppies huddled under the garden bench could just be seen by the gas light.

"Wait just a moment," Charlie said, stepping back into the kitchen.

I, being of course impervious to rain and common sense, did not wait. The garden gate was closed and there was nowhere for the puppies to run, so I knelt in front of them and held out my hand.

"Hello there, lads. A rather dreary night for you to be out, isn't it?"

One of the pups was shaggy and had the look of a terrier or a wolfhound, and the other was a short-haired black breed with enormous paws. They shivered together and shrank back from my hand. Charlie knelt down beside me and handed me a bit of cold meat pie from lunch, then held her own piece out to the black puppy, which was closest to her, and spoke in quiet, soothing tones.

"Well, aren't you the lovely pup who has been playing outside my window? Do you have no one to bring you in at night, you sweet thing?"

The black puppy inched forward toward the meat pie in her hand, while the shaggy one hung back out of range of my hand to see what happened. Charlie kept speaking.

"You're such a brave dog, look how smart you are to come into our garden for shelter. Brave puppies get treats and baths and lovely fires to keep them warm." The puppy crawled out from under the bench, and gently took the bit of meat pie from Charlie's hand. She left her fingers just where they'd been, and when the puppy sniffed her fingers, and then licked them, she slowly moved to scratch behind his ears.

While I'd been watching the black pup take food from my wife, the shaggy one had crawled forward and was carefully sniffing the food in my hand. By the time he'd eaten it and received his own ear scratches, the black pup was cradled in Charlie's arms. She looked at me with a spectacular smile, rain running down her face and a muddy puppy staining the front of her dress.

"We're keeping them, aren't we?" she asked.

The shaggy puppy crawled his way into my lap, soaking my trousers with mud and wet dog. I laughed at the picture we made. "I think they're keeping us," I said.

Later, when the puppies we named Gryf and Huff were washed and drying in a nest of towels by the kitchen fire, Charlie and I sat on the floor next to them, nursing cups of tea.

"We managed to keep Mrs. Mac's kitchen floor clean," Charlie said, looking around us with a giggle.

"She said that, didn't she? *Her* kitchen floor," I marveled.

"Do you think she'll fuss about the dogs?" Charlie asked.

I laughed and shook my head. "She knew we'd bring them inside. I think she wanted us to."

Charlie ran her fingers through Huff's shaggy fur, and he sighed contentedly in his sleep. "I like her. After the disaster with the 'get out' woman, I didn't want anyone else to come into our house. But I think Mrs. Mac knows we're different, and it doesn't seem to matter."

I shrugged and stared into the fire. "Different is about what someone *isn't*, and therefore has no value as a measure of character. If I had to guess, Mrs. Mac is not one to measure character based on how things appear."

"She is so wonderfully tall," Charlie sighed, "and quite stylish."

I smiled at my petite wife who always admired height for the advantages it gave. "She takes evident care with her appearance, and quite likely will take equal care of our house."

We spent the evening moving more of the drawing room furniture, and Charlie took particular care making sure Mrs. Mac's bedroom and sitting room were comfortable. I rigged a gas stove with the facilities to heat water, similar to what I'd done in my hidden flat, and we dragged a large tub into the basement room near the housekeeper's quarters.

We worked late into the night, woke the puppies for a trip outside to the garden, then settled them back into their bed by the kitchen fire when we finally trudged up to our bed. We slept until nearly eleven, and when we finally emerged downstairs, it was to find that Mrs. Mac had somehow let herself in – I clearly needed to change the locks – and fed the puppies, which now cavorted outside in the garden, washed and waxed the entry hall floor, polished a ridiculous amount of silver, filled vases with winter greenery, and was just pulling a loaf of fresh bread from the oven.

She looked up as we came in. "Good morning, Mr. and Mrs. Devereux. I trust you slept well?"

"We did, Mrs. Mac. I'm sorry we're so late to breakfast," Charlie said with chagrin.

"Nonsense," Mrs. Mac said gruffly. "The kettle is on, the bread is fresh, and when you let the puppies back in, please make sure you wipe their feet, Mr. Devereux."

With the puppies properly introduced to our new housekeeper and settled into their basket by the fire, Charlie and I sat across from each other at the big wooden kitchen table drinking tea and eating fresh bread. We discussed a market Charlie had seen that she wondered if I'd like to join her in exploring, and I suggested a stop at the stationers for more art supplies, and all the while Mrs. Mac bustled in the background, preparing the stock for a soup while organizing the butler's pantry.

Finally, after we'd consumed the last of the tea, she stood in front of us and said, in the first awkwardness I'd seen from her, "I … thank you for making my rooms downstairs so comfortable."

We looked at her in surprise, and Charlie said, "Please don't feel you need to keep anything we put there, and in fact, if there's anything else in the house that appeals to you, we're happy to discuss it."

"The only thing—" again, oddly, her tone lacked confidence. "Would you please show me how to heat the water for the bath? I've never—" she cleared her throat "—that is, none of my other accommodations ever had a private bath."

"Of course," I said. "I'd be happy to show you how it works. I designed a system like it for our old flat by the docks, and I'm available to show you anytime."

She cleared her throat again and went back to bustling efficiency. "I appreciate the courtesy very much."

I pulled handful of sovereign coins from my pocket. "We prefer to pay upfront for our expenses," I said, handing her the coins. "This will do until we can get to the bank, but then you and Charlie should sit down with the account books to figure out what you'll need to run the house properly."

Mrs. Mac took the coins, but her voice betrayed her surprise. "What is it you do for your living, Mr. Devereux?"

I chuckled ruefully and met Charlie's eyes. "At the moment, nothing. We inherited the house, and the means to fund it, but we haven't yet figured out what to be when we grow up."

Charlie was rather unsuccessful at hiding her smile, so she spoke to cover it. "We've been accepted to King's College and intend to enroll as students."

Mrs. Mac's mouth dropped open. "Well, isn't that grand," she said without a trace of irony. "University for the both of you. What'll you study?"

"Everything," I said earnestly, at the same time as Charlie said, "History."

I looked at Charlie in surprise. I guess I'd assumed she would study art, especially after the lessons she'd taken with a master painter at the Grayson Estate.

Charlie met my eyes. "So many things can be learned from other people's stories."

I picked her hand up from the table and kissed her fingertips as she smiled at me. "Things like tolerance and empathy," I added, "and the history we learn so as not to repeat it."

"I read about the horrors of war when I was young, and knew I could never be a soldier," Mrs. Mac said with a shudder, in what felt like a remarkably unguarded statement for a woman of such discretion.

"I find love stories to be the most valuable," Charlie said, "because they're full of hope. And with hope, anything is possible."

I kept Charlie's hand and helped her to her feet. "My love, grab your hat and gloves, and when I've shown Mrs. Mac the secrets of her hot water, you and I will go down to King's College to see about registering for our first classes."

She beamed at me. "That sounds like a perfect excuse for an outing," she said before thanking Mrs. Mac for breakfast and departing the room.

I turned to our new housekeeper and lowered my voice. "Mrs. Mac, first, I need to apologize to you. I am sometimes arrogant in my observations, and it was never my intention to cause you discomfort."

She looked taken-aback. "Mr. Devereux, I am abrasive and taciturn to a fault. If you can allow me to remain thus, I shall certainly allow your rather well-deserved arrogance."

It was my turn to be startled. "In that case, I need some silver. Is there a pure silver spoon or fork in our collection that could be sacrificed to my cause?"

She looked sharply at me as I cleared our dishes to the sink and attempted to wash them. "I'll thank you to let me do my job, sir. And I thought you inherited funds."

"Please don't address me as 'sir.' It doesn't fit the person I believe myself to be."

Mrs. Mac's eyebrow rose and the barest hint of mirth quirked her mouth. I continued with a chuckle at my own expense. "Ringo is fine, and it's not for the money," I said. "I need the silver element. Come to think of it, I also need a bit of space where I can ignite zinc and sulfur."

She narrowed her eyes at me. "Is that how it's going to be then? University students doing experiments and mixing compounds? You'll not be doing that in my kitchen," she huffed. "There's a room off the wine cellar downstairs that you can use if you must."

"Thank you, Mrs. Mac," I said. "You can show me the room after I've explained your hot water. And I promise not to stink up the whole house."

"See that you don't," she muttered under her breath, "Ringo." I caught her quick smile to herself, and I was remarkably glad that she had joined our household.

After visits to both the Strand campus of King's College and the Kensington Square building that housed the Ladies Department of King's College, and several quiet games of "Deduction" about other pedestrians as we walked, I ducked into the Geological Society of London to buy the minerals I required. Charlie was curious, but merely smiled and shook her head at me when I said it was a surprise.

We stopped at Rothschild & Sons bank to meet the director and confirm our account, and I tried and failed not to blink at the amount of money Archer and Saira had made available to us. I wanted to write a thank you note to leave in the safe deposit box, but Charlie reminded me that they'd be called when the box was checked in their time, so we should make it count with a longer letter containing all our news about the puppies and Mrs. Mac and enrollment in our colleges instead.

After a wonderful roast chicken dinner prepared by Mrs. Mac and an evening spent playing with the puppies by the library fire, I kissed Charlie goodnight and sent her upstairs to bed. "It's a surprise," I said, and a look of wonder and possibly trepidation entered my wife's eyes, but she kissed me and went to bed anyway.

Mrs. Mac directed me to a cellar room with a window and a basin of water, where I could grind the zinc and sulfur into powder, ignite them, and then melt the silver spoon into the mix. She left the door open as she walked down the hall to her own quarters, muttering in vaguely Scottish noises about students and experiments and fires, and I silently vowed not to blow up the house, or indeed, cause much of a stink at all.

The next day, after my walk in the park with the dogs, I bought a tin of paint and smuggled it into the cellar. Then, while Charlie and Mrs. Mac worked out recipes and schedules and probably plotted world domination, I locked myself in the ballroom and got to work.

That night, after a lovely conversation Mrs. Mac pretended not to join as she prepared bread dough nearby while adding several insightful comments, and after Gryf and Huff, having wrestled each other into exhaustion, were nuzzled, cuddled, and then safely ensconced in their kitchen basket, I guided my wife, not to the library as was our custom in the evenings, but to the ballroom.

I covered her eyes and led her inside, and when she could finally see what I'd done, she gasped and laughed and cried in such rapid succession, I fell in love with her all over again.

"Oh Ringo, it's beautiful," she said, her eyes glowing in the light of a hundred candles. "Just like our flat, but in a space that requires no silence." She toed off her shoes and spun in a circle, her arms outstretched, her head thrown back, and her eyes closed in blissful joy. "Do you know," she said, meeting my admiring gaze, "now that Mrs. Mac has joined us and the puppies have taken over, this place has begun to feel like a home. I think any house we live in will always need lots of life to fill the silences." Charlie's smile was so full of pure happiness that my heart felt three sizes too big for my chest.

Finally, my wife sank into the nest of pillows and rugs I'd made in the center of the ballroom floor and patted the space beside her. "Lie next to me," she said. I stepped inside the circle of candlelight, and lay down on my back, holding my arm out for her to do the same. When she nestled into my chest, she finally looked up at the zinc, sulfur, and silver luminescent paint that dotted the ceiling.

"Stars," she whispered as she turned to me, "You gave me stars."

"I just showed them where we live," I said with a smile, as I saw the warm light of our home shining in her eyes.

But Wait, There's More...

Thank you for joining Ringo and Charlie on their journey through the Immortal Descendants tales and beyond. It was a joy to pick up the threads of their story and weave them together for this book, and I hope they made you smile a little as Ringo and Charlie found their way forward.

A special and heartfelt thanks to Kathleen Menninger, whose insight and wisdom are matched only by her incredible generosity, and to Franziska Stern, whose creativity and talent as a cover designer breathed fresh inspiration into this series. As always, this book would not exist without my spectacular friend and editor, Angela Houle. Truly, there aren't enough words in the definition of "brilliant" to do her justice.

Ahead is the first chapter of *An Urchin of Means*, currently available in ebook, paperback, and an incomparable audiobook narrated by Will Watt. Urchin begins about eight months after the end of *A House Called Home*, and book two of the Baker Street Mysteries, *A Lady in Waiting*, will be releasing soon. Please enjoy Ringo's adventures as the unintentional inspiration for Sherlock Holmes.

An Urchin of Means

Chapter 1 – Thief

The little guttersnipe was fast, I'd give it that.

Quick-fingered and fleet-footed, for all it was ten years old, and there I'd been, cutting across Regent's Park with my arms full of books as if I were the most oblivious nob in London. Damn, but I was in no mood to run. The entire month of August had been hot, and the camouflage I wore – the well-cut coat and fussy cravat of a respectable university student – was stifling. But if I didn't tuck the books away somewhere and sprint after it, I'd lose Charlie's money, and I certainly did not want to tell my wife the advance for her illustrations had been lifted from my pocket by a street rat.

The thief clearly hadn't expected me to give chase. It was of indeterminate gender, small, slender, barefoot, and wearing its own camouflage of street grime. Grime was different than filth – grime coated the skin and clothes with good, clean dirt but didn't smell of sewers or sweat. Filth stank and made people wary, therefore proper pickpockets tended to be fairly fastidious in their grooming habits under the dirt.

My annoyance grew in direct proportion to the distance we covered, and despite my longer legs, this rat had remarkable stamina. It took a turn out of the land of the quite-well-off, and darted into the dangerous territory of the very well-to-do, where the degrees of wealth ran from having one country manor to having ten. I hadn't called out for help yet – my own habit toward invisibility being too ingrained – but when the street rat sprinted toward the Langham Hotel, I finally knew how to trap it.

"Stop! Thief!"

My voice had a pleasing boom and caused people to look around for the big man they assumed must go with it. I was not overly tall – early years of hunger had likely stunted what may have been a large frame if I'd had proper feeding – but my voice had become surprisingly deep. It was menacing when I needed it to be, and authoritative enough to let me blend into the wealthy clientele of the Langham.

A slightly startled doorman, sporting the name John Hartwell on his uniform, acted without thought and grabbed my thief as she – yes, upon closer examination of delicate collar bones and elfin features, the street rat appeared to be female – attempted to slip into the hotel. I had perhaps ten seconds before Hartwell thought better of holding such a wriggly little thing and let her go; ten seconds in which to proclaim my authority over the glaring creature and retrieve Charlie's money. The shreds of my own dignity, as a pickpocket's victim, would be less simple to recover.

"Right. I'll just have my wallet back then," I said to the creature as I approached.

"I ain't got nothin' of yers," she snarled back, squirming violently in the doorman's hands.

I ignored her and met Hartwell's startled eyes. He was surprised, perhaps, that I was young and lean and didn't fit the voice I'd used to command the rat's capture. "I'll take this little vermin off your hands and remove it from your very fine establishment, if you please?" I slid into a posh, upper-crust accent – I'd been practicing such mimicry for months, and it had become frighteningly second-nature. As such things still did in the English class system, the cadence of expensive English boarding school had the desired effect. It baffled me that such a simple thing as an accent could induce a person to compliance, and yet the evidence was right in front of me.

"Right-o, Guv." Hartwell shoved the pickpocket forward, and she stumbled into my hands. She tried to wrench herself away before I could get a solid grip on her bony shoulders, but I had her spun around, one arm twisted up behind her back, before she could so much as spit, which I expected would have come next if I had been so foolish as to face her.

"All right, Rat. Out you go," I murmured into her ear as I marched her through the door and back out to the street.

"I'm no rat," she protested sharply as she attempted to bite the arm I'd wrapped across her shoulders.

"If it scurries like a rat, and squeaks like a rat, it must be a rat. The question is whether you'll escape this particular trap intact. That was my wife's money you stole, and I'll have it back now."

The girl scoffed. "'Whoever 'eard of a wife with 'er own bob? It all belongs to ye, don't it?"

"It is money she *earned*. Perhaps even you can appreciate the significance of that." I had my coin purse from the band at her waist and tucked into my trouser pocket before she felt the slightest motion. Despite having been ridiculously careless enough to get pickpocketed in the first place, my own dexterity, which had fed me for much of my early life, remained firmly habitual.

"'Ere now! That's mine ye be takin'!" Her voice screeched alarmingly, and for one quick moment I feared she would draw heroic eyes to her plight. Doormen I could reason with, but men or women of the social justice warrior class were more than I had patience for in the London heat with a wriggling pickpocket in my hands.

I leaned close to her ear and dropped my voice to a menacing snarl, adopting the most effective accent for the job. "Ye'll 'ear this once, and only once. Marylebone is mine. From Regent's Park to Mayfair and Fitzrovia, the only nimble-fingered guttersnipes that work 'ere work fer me. And since ye don't work fer me, *ye don't work 'ere.*"

The girl had frozen for exactly one second at the knife's edge in my voice, then gave up her struggle as a bad job. She wasn't afraid of me, but perhaps my accent had convinced her I wasn't quite the nob she'd first believed. My awareness of the street around us had grown more pronounced as I spoke – the sounds of horses' hooves told me the carriage that had pulled up behind me was driven by four spry

Morgans, one of which was going lame. Conversations around us quickly catalogued themselves in my brain as important, like the young man gossiping with another about a scandalous baccarat game attended by the prince, or trivial, like the wife accusing her husband of appreciating another woman. And ringing above it all was the jangle of coins in a man's pocket that included the dull ring of a solid gold sovereign. I knew the rat had heard all these things as well, and I wondered if perhaps I should make a point of behaving like a tough for a few minutes each day to stay sharp.

The lunch crowd was beginning to thicken the street with the posh and powerful who regularly dined at places such as the Langham. I pulled the girl away from the hotel entrance toward Portland Place. We turned the corner to avoid a couple approaching the steps and nearly collided with a tall man in a frock coat who walked with the long stride of the very confident.

"Ringo, my dear young man! How lovely to see you!" The man's deep, cultured voice was instantly recognizable, though it had the unfortunate effect of jolting my concentration. The rat jerked her arm free, and I succeeded in catching only a bit of the collar of her shirt, which neatly disintegrated with age.

I looked up to find the enormously amused Oscar Wilde smiling down at me. "Oh dear, I do hope I didn't frighten that poor child away from whatever nefarious task you had planned for the creature," he said cheerfully.

"*She* had just successfully picked my pocket. I was merely attempting to restore a shred of my professional dignity while relieving her of the ill-gotten gain," I said as I straightened the infernal cravat.

"Your professional dignity?" Wilde ventured.

I spoke the truth with just enough humor in my tone as to render it unbelievable. "Evidently, my previous life as a thief and pickpocket didn't leave identifying marks."

Wilde's booming laughter at my apparent joke carried to the front doors of the Langham, in the direction of which he was suddenly propelling me. "Come to lunch with me. I'm meeting two other gentlemen of the storytelling persuasion, and they will wish to hear the tale of your adventure as much as I."

I thought of my books, hidden behind a bench in Regent's Park, and I thought of the long walk in the blazing midday sun to retrieve them before my planned expedition to study at the University College library, where I'd spent the past year being a respectable student of philosophy and physics, with enough history, science, and letters to keep things entertaining.

I held my hand out to shake, and it was instantly enveloped in his ridiculously large, yet remarkably gentle grip. "I'm delighted to see you again, Mr. Wilde. I was on my way to study physics, but I believe the restoration of my dignity might require a thoroughly self-effacing recounting of the day's events. Thank you for the invitation."

He clapped me on the shoulder. "Good man! Education is an admirable thing, but it is well to remember from time to time that nothing that is worth knowing can be taught. And if it assuages your conscience, I am certain there was an element of physics at play in the encounter with your thief."

I chuckled as I recalled an image of the street rat dropping off a wall, tumbling down an embankment, and leaping a leashed bulldog that turned and snapped at her heels. She was resourceful and intrepid — qualities I rarely had the occasion to admire among my recent acquaintances.

"Indeed, there was." I looked back over my shoulder for the young thief I knew was long gone, and then allowed myself to be directed back into the elegant foyer of the Langham Hotel.

An Urchin of Means is available in ebook and paperback from Amazon and on all other platforms.

APRIL WHITE has been a film producer, private investigator, bouncer, teacher and screenwriter. She has climbed in the Himalayas, survived a shipwreck, and lived on a gold mine in the Yukon. She and her husband share their home in Southern California with two extraordinary, nearly-grown children and a lifetime collection of books.

Her first novel, *Marking Time* is the 2016 winner of the Library Journal Indie E-Book Award for YA Literature, and all five books in the Immortal Descendants series have been on the Amazon Top 100 lists in Time Travel Romance and Historical Fantasy. Her romantic suspense novel, *Code of Conduct* is an RWA Vivian Award finalist, a Next Generation Award finalist, and RONE Award finalist. And her time travel sci-fi novella, *Death's Door* is a Grand Prize winner of the Next Generation Award, winner of the Edgar Allen Poe Festival Saturday Visiter Award, and a Foreword Reviews Award finalist.

More information and her blog can be found at aprilwhitebooks.com.